MW00413210

A Life Such as Heaven Intended

A Novel

By Amanda Lauer

Full Quiver Publishing
Pakenham, Ontario

This book is a work of fiction. Although the setting for this novel takes place in the 19th century, some of the names, characters and incidents are products of the author's imagination. Real events and characters are used fictitiously.

A Life Such as Heaven Intended
copyright 2018
by Amanda Lauer

Published by Full Quiver Publishing
PO Box 244
Pakenham, Ontario K0A 2X0

ISBN Number: 978-1-987970-09-8
Printed and bound in the USA

Background cover photo: David Haack
Back cover photo: Anna Coltran of Belle Gente Photography
Cover design: James Hrkach

NATIONAL LIBRARY OF CANADA
CATALOGUING IN PUBLICATION

Copyright 2018 by Amanda Lauer
Published by Full Quiver Publishing
A Division of Innate Productions

To Stephanie, Nicholas, Samantha and Elizabeth

In my life, I love you more

Thou are sleeping, brother, sleeping
In thy lonely battle grave;
Shadows o'er the past are creeping,
Death, the reaper, still is reaping,
Years have swept and years are sweeping,
Many a memory from my keeping,
But I'm waiting still, and weeping
For my beautiful and brave.

~ In Memoriam, David J. Ryan, C.S.A.
By Father Abraham Ryan, Poet Priest of the Confederacy

Chapter I

Wednesday, May 25, 1864

Dallas, Georgia

She bolted upright in the four-poster bed, the chain-spring mattress squeaking in protest. Her heart pounded in her chest as she surveyed the bedroom, searching for the source of the noise that woke her from her early morning slumber.

The sun was just cresting the horizon and offered enough light for her to look over every item in her room — the table, wardrobe, a small bookcase filled to overflowing with tomes in various colors and sizes, the chest of drawers, washstand, mahogany Empire chair, tall mirror and chaise lounge. Everything appeared to be exactly where it belonged.

Yet Brigid McGinnis swore she had heard a scraping noise. It was the same sound that came to her ears sporadically in the wee hours of the morning when she was home for breaks from the Lucy Cobb Institute. Curiously, as far back as she could remember, she heard the noise intermittently — it never seemed to occur when her father was in residence at their house.

John Thaddeus McGinnis spent little time in his hometown of Dallas since the troubles between the states began. As the owner of Hamilton State Bank, and caretaker of the old money secured for the well-heeled families in town, he had been asked by President Jefferson Davis to be a member of his cabinet when Davis was elected president of the Confederate States of America in February of 1861.

Her father had declined the offer at the time because of family and business obligations. His wife, Brigid's mother,

Catherine Agatha Murphy McGinnis, was expecting their fourth child and was confined to her bed for the last three months of her term. Mrs. McGinnis was insistent that her husband stay in Dallas until the child was born. In addition, with the talk of war heating up, Mr. McGinnis felt obliged to maintain his position at the helm of the institution he ran. His clients were getting skittish, and he wanted to do everything he could to avoid a run on the bank.

When the War Between the States was declared on April 12, 1861, Mr. McGinnis pledged his allegiance to the Confederate States. He had no intention of taking up arms because, at thirty-seven, not only was he too old, but he was no longer in fighting form after years of indulging in the finer things of life. But in July of that year, when his wife was safely delivered of their son, John Thaddeus McGinnis II, Mr. McGinnis accepted the position of Secretary of the Interior of the Confederate States of America.

Mrs. McGinnis oversaw the household staff when her husband was on official duty in Richmond and she ran a tight ship. Had she not been a female, she would have been well-suited for a career as a naval officer. When she snapped her fingers, the servants scurried to do her bidding, as did Mr. McGinnis.

The arrangement of balancing his position with the Confederate government and running his bank worked well until *That Day*, as Brigid referred to it, in January of 1862. Ever since *That Day,* things had changed dramatically for their family and in their house. She didn't like to think of it and did her best to brush it out of her mind whenever it crept to the forefront of her cranium. From *That Day* on, her father spent as little time at their house as possible and threw himself into his work for the Confederacy.

Shaking her head to clear those thoughts, Brigid strained to hear the noise again. A shiver went down her spine. *Why am I the only one who ever hears this?* Her mother and two younger sisters shared sleeping quarters on the other side of the house. Agnes was eight and Martha was six years old. Brigid didn't want to frighten them so she only voiced her concerns to her mother. The woman dismissed her unease, noting she had never heard anything out of the ordinary at night or any other time of the day for that matter.

That really didn't surprise Brigid. Ever since *That Day*, her mother, who until that point had always shown such affection for her oldest daughter, hadn't been herself. It was as though the wind had been taken out of her sails. Where she once ruled the household with military precision, she now had little passion for her duties. She had turned most of the day-to-day operations over to Beulah, the head cook, who watched over the household unless Brigid was home — then that task fell to her. She may as well have been hired help herself for as much notice her mother took of her endeavors.

Regardless, Brigid wished she could ease more of the burden from her mother's shoulders, but her studies kept her up in Athens for a good portion of the year, except during school breaks. A week ago, she graduated from Lucy Cobb, but she didn't intend to stay at the house long — her father was in the process of making plans for her future. His standards were quite rigid, so it could take him several months to sort through the options. Once his mind was made up, Brigid knew her fate would be sealed, and she would be heading to a new town to start the next phase of her life.

Brigid sat still and listened intently. No other sound was forthcoming, so she wrote it off as a product of her overactive imagination. She laid her head back down on the feather pillow and closed her eyes to try and get another hour or so of sleep. With everything going on around her lately, she had so much to worry about that her slumber had been restless. Many a morning she awoke feeling more tired than she had been when she went to bed the night before.

Like a China doll with eyes painted wide open, Brigid's eyelids refused to shut. She stared up at the fleur-de-lis patterned fabric draped over the top of the bed posts. Once her brain woke up, she couldn't stop the thoughts from racing through her head.

The troubles drew closer and closer to their door. For the past several days, she heard the sound of gunfire just outside town. As much as her parents had done to shelter her and her siblings from news about the war, Brigid had ears, and she heard the whispers amongst the parishioners at The Church of the Purification of the Blessed Virgin Mary. She saw the bulletins being nailed to the trees in the town square with the latest lists of the dead and missing soldiers from their area. Try as she might to ignore them, the voices of the men on the lists drew her over to the square. She would read each name and say a prayer for the man's soul with the hope that some of the lost would be found. However, the number of young men she saw out and about town dwindled each day as if they were weeds being plucked from well-manicured lawns.

She did not like being the one in charge of their household, even if it was temporary. Brigid wasn't brave by any means — she was afraid of countless things including lightning, insects, horses, mice, and the damp and dark root cellar of their house. Even Agnes was braver than she was — it was her job to kill any errant spiders Brigid encountered in the house.

The thought of facing something as menacing as a troop of Union soldiers frightened the wits out of her. There was no place to hide on their property so they'd be forced to flee, but where would they find shelter? The McGinnis family lived on the outskirts of town, so they didn't have any neighbors nearby to help them.

If only her mother would be her old self again — that spirited lady would know exactly what to do. Any Union soldiers who went toe to toe with the former Mrs. McGinnis would be well advised to turn on their heels and run. She would set them in their place so fast their heads would spin. *Maybe that was what the South needed to finally put this affair to rest — a regiment of strong-backed women like her mother to let the Union Army know what's what.*

Seeing that it was useless to continue lying in bed when she was wide awake, and knowing there were things she could be doing, Brigid got up and went to the wardrobe to fetch her dressing gown. She slipped it on and then opened her bedroom door and headed down the hallway to the front staircase.

Normally she wouldn't be caught dead walking through the house with nightclothes on, but it wasn't even five o'clock in the morning, so none of the staff members were up for the day. She wanted to go outside and pump water from the well to start a pot of hickory coffee. Her mother had often told her that coffee was for adults and not young ladies but seeing that Brigid was taking on grown-up responsibilities she felt she ought to get some of the rewards as well. Anyhow, she would be turning eighteen in just over eight months, so she was on the cusp of adulthood.

She just wished they had real coffee grounds for a cup of the black coffee like Beulah used to make before the war started. She missed that smell; it seemed like forever since they'd had any. The shipping lanes for the Confederate states had been blocked the last two years and no exports were making their way to the northern part of the state.

Thinking of the aromatic scent of that Jamaican coffee brought back memories of the years before the war began.

After the spring of 1861, life changed dramatically for every person Brigid knew. They used to have parties and balls and picnics. All the ladies and gentlemen of good esteem wanted to be seen at her family's house. Gentlefolk throughout the county coveted invitations to events her parents hosted.

Her father was wont to work nonstop, but her mother lived by the axiom that all work and no play made Mr. McGinnis a dull boy. She insisted on keeping a full social calendar for both of them. That included not only throwing lavish soirées but making their appearance at other gatherings that kept their social standing elevated to its appropriate level. Whatever plans Mrs. McGinnis made, Mr. McGinnis was obligated to attend. He lived by the maxim, "Happy wife, happy life."

Brigid sighed as she remembered the many festivities her parents had hosted. She prayed that someday things would return to normal and they could resume their old lives. Thinking further on that, she realized that couldn't possibly happen for her because her future plans didn't include any parties — most certainly not the debutante ball she always thought she'd have.   Do women religious celebrate anything other than holy days?

Shrugging her shoulders, Brigid walked to the kitchen and grabbed the kettle off the shelf. She then quietly opened the door behind her that led to the backyard and headed down the back steps. Once in the yard the dew made the grass a bit slippery under her bare feet so she watched her footing as she hurried to the hand pump.

It took a good six pumps to start the water trickling from the well but then two more pumps and it was flowing briskly. Brigid filled the kettle and leaned forward to get a drink of the cool, refreshing water.

When she was done, she turned and started back to the house. By this time the sun was peeking over the neighbor's field. It looked like they were in for a hot, sunny day — it would be tempting to stay in her dressing gown for the entire day. It was much cooler than the long-sleeved, high necked dress and hoops in which her handmaid would dress her later. But that would not be acceptable. At least Tilly would pin her hair up after she was dressed so she would be a little cooler. It was a painstaking process because her hair was so long and thick, but it would be worth it.

Brigid lifted her gaze and stopped dead in her tracks. Something lay next to the back left corner of the house. Keeping her distance, she took three large steps sideways to see if she could make out what it was. She prayed it wasn't a dog because she was afraid of them too. With the shortage of food in the area lately, her limbs, as skinny as they were, would look like warm and juicy drumsticks to a hungry mongrel.

Squinting, she could see that the object was too big to be a dog. She took two steps closer and dropped the kettle to the ground, causing water to splash under her gown all the way to her calves.

Good Lord, it was a human being! More precisely, as she noted after cautiously taking one step closer, it was a man and he wore a Confederate uniform. Her mind raced as she considered the picture before her. *What would cause a soldier to lie down in our backyard,* she wondered as the thumping of her heart resounded in her head.

Brigid had heard about soldiers deserting their posts and making their way back to their hometowns. Some had honorable intentions — they had farms that needed tending or a new baby to greet, but some were downright dangerous — they were so desperate to get out of the line of fire they would cut down anything in their path that threatened to stop their escape.

If the man was a deserter, he could have easily concealed

himself inside their barn rather than choose such a conspicuous place to rest. Or was he resting? He wasn't moving a muscle. Was he asleep, unconscious, or — God forbid — dead.

Inching nearer, she could see his chest slowly rising and falling. Brigid exhaled in relief. She tiptoed close enough to give him a more thorough look-over. He wore butternut colored trousers with a dark blue stripe running along the outside seam of the leg and a matching single-breasted wool jacket that was adorned with dark blue-braided trim. He clutched a piece of headwear, possibly a slouch hat like many of the enlisted men wore.

While it was hard to determine accurately since he was lying on the ground, Brigid guessed him to be of average height for a man — which would be a good six inches taller than she. He looked to be around her age, maybe a couple of years older at the most.

His build was quite muscular, not like the scrawny boys she was accustomed to seeing around town. The mop of brown hair was a few shades lighter than her own. Mrs. McGinnis called Brigid's hair color chestnut, which sounded exotic, but when she glanced in the looking glass all she saw was saw ordinary brown hair, similar in color to the mane of the horses in her father's barn.

Thank goodness no one was around because Brigid couldn't help but gawk at the man's handsome facade. Something about his features made her heart pound even faster than it had moments earlier. He had black eyelashes that were sinfully long for a man and eyebrows the same hue as his hair. She couldn't help but wonder what color his eyes were. He had dark skin — whether it was from the sun or his heritage, it was hard to say. Stubble covered his rugged square jaw. Stepping in a bit closer, the color drained from her cheeks. There was dried blood in his hair, and he had a gash extending from his temple to behind his right ear.

A sense of compassion overtook her, and she had to hold herself back to keep from touching her fingertips to his forehead. She looked him over and tried to determine what her next step would be, but she didn't get far in her ruminations. In the blink of an eye, a hand streaked out and wrapped around her ankle like a steel vice. Brigid let out a yelp and almost tripped over herself trying to get away, but she was trapped.

Chapter II

His hand was clamped onto something, but he wasn't sure exactly what he had captured since he could hardly open his eyes. Whatever it was, it seemed desperate to get away.

The man scrunched his eyes shut and then tried opening them completely. He saw his arm fully extended in front of him just inches above a plot of grass. It appeared he was grasping onto an ankle, a slim porcelain-colored one at that.

He had no idea why he was hanging onto that appendage for dear life, but something must have compelled him to do that. Attached to the petite ankle was an equally petite bare foot. His gaze traveled up and he saw a flowing white silk garment, perhaps a dressing gown of some sorts.

Sunlight hit his eyes, so he had to squint as he glanced further upward. Bewildered, he shook his head slightly.

"Are you an angel?" he asked as he perused the extraordinary features of the beauty he held in his grasp. He could not get over the color of her eyes — he had never seen such a shade before. They were the color of emeralds and glittered like gemstones too.

There was no answer other than a tug and a grunt as the female tried to extract herself from his bondage.

"Is this heaven?" Still hanging onto the ankle, he lifted his head and looked around at the yard and flower gardens.

He got his answer soon enough.

For a petite thing, that chit had some power in her. Her toe struck his funny bone dead on, and the force made him let go of her ankle.

Nein, definitive kein Engle, he thought.

"Most certainly not an angel," said the man out loud, bringing his right hand around to rub his elbow. "Well, maybe a fallen angel."

A look of astonishment crossed the creature's comely face. Now that she had stepped away, the man could see it was a young lady, perhaps in her late teen years. She backed up and nearly tripped over a hoe lying on the ground near the flowerbed. She bent down and picked it up and then advanced closer to him but kept well out of arm's reach.

"Who...who are you?" she asked, her voice shaking as she brandished the hoe with two hands in front of her. "And why are you in my father's yard?"

Those were two very good questions. It vexed him that he couldn't answer them. He gingerly tried to push himself up into a sitting position. He ached from head to toe. The woman shook her head in a warning and took a step nearer to him.

"Don't do anything foolish." She pointed the hoe at his skull.

Since his head was already throbbing, he suspected he had taken a blow to the noggin — perhaps at the young lady's hands? That was doubtful; as petite as she was, he couldn't imagine that she packed much of a punch. He attempted to remember but, try as he might, nothing was coming to him. He held his hands in the air in a show of surrender.

"Ich gebe auf."

"What is that supposed to mean?" she stammered.

"It means, I don't know. You can try beating it out of me, but I don't have the foggiest idea what my name is or how I ended up on your father's property. Who is your father, anyway?"

"I'm the one asking questions, not you," said the girl in a shaky voice.

"Well, you can ask all you want, but if I can't even remember the most basic information about myself, I would think anything beyond that would stump me."

The little lady didn't seem to believe his story. She looked around as if trying to determine her next course of action.

"Do you have any identification?" she asked warily.

"That's another fine question, miss. I really don't know. Would you like to check?" he asked solicitously.

"I'm not going to touch you," she said indignantly. "Check yourself and be quick about it. The servants will be rising soon. They'll wonder why I'm harboring a fugitive in the perennial garden."

Her accent was enchanting. She looked at him expectantly, waiting for an answer.

He blinked his eyes a few times to regain his focus. "I would find it highly unlikely that I am a fugitive." He stuffed his right hand into the various pockets of his outerwear. "If I were, I suspect I'd be better at it and not be hiding in wide open view."

Keeping one hand in the air, he opened the front of his jacket. There was something in the interior pocket. The object was small but relatively thick. Pulling it out, he discovered a book with the words, *Die Heilige Schrift*, scripted on the cover.

He held it up for the young lady's inspection.

"What does it say?" she inquired.

"The Holy Bible," he translated. That was odd, he thought. Instinctively, he knew he was speaking English with the young lady, but German phrases were at the tip of his tongue and, apparently, he had the ability to read the language as well. Maybe that bit of information would open the curtains to his mind and help him recall how he happened to be in this particular set of circumstances.

"Is there an inscription?"

The man opened the front cover and turned the first page. On the left-hand side was indeed an inscription written in faded ink. Most of the script was too light to read but he was able to decipher the first word.

"Dominic," he said out loud.

"Is that your name then – Dominic?"

Dominic. It sounded so sweet coming from her lips that he'd be willing to change his name if it wasn't.

"I'll be darned if I know." He shrugged his shoulders. "But if it's not, I'm not sure how that fellow's Bible came to be in my possession."

Now that he thought of it, that name did sound familiar. He let the word sink into his mind for a few seconds. Closing his eyes, he listened, trying to recall if that might be the name to which he was accustomed to answering.

A flash came to him. *Flames surrounded him. Desperate to find something, he crawled through the loft of a small wooden house with a shake roof. Clutching his Bible in one hand, he searched through the hay scattered on the floor. A pitiful meowing came from nearby. His heart leaping with hope, he scrambled on hands and knees toward the source of the sound. A door slammed downstairs.*

In the back of his mind he could hear a woman calling out that name. She called it over and over with a frantic tone in her voice. Thinking harder he remembered something. *The woman came rushing through the door of the house and started climbing the ladder to the loft area.*

"Kommen Zie," she yelled. He ignored her command as he was determined to find the animal. When the lady got

to the top of the ladder she crawled into the loft towards him, grabbed a hold of his shirttail and pulled him to the edge of the space.

A stocky man rushed into the dwelling and got on the ladder and reached towards the woman. She pushed him towards the ladder and into the man's arms. The man dropped him to the floor and firmly said, "Ausführen!" He was paralyzed with fear. "Schnell! Schnell!" Obeying, he finally turned and scampered out the door.

Once outside, he ran across the yard and then stopped to look behind him. To his horror he saw the roof collapsing, and he knew the man and the woman were trapped inside the building. He tried to go into the structure, but the flames were too intense.

His eyes flew open. "*Ich bin* Dominic," he said quietly.

Seeing no look of comprehension on the young lady's face, he repeated himself in English. "I am Dominic."

She still looked apprehensive but politely replied back. "My name is Brigid...Brigid McGinnis. How do you do?"

She was obviously a young woman with an impeccable upbringing.

The girl looked at him curiously as though she really was concerned and wasn't just being cordial.

"I've seen better days, but I do believe things are on the upswing," he noted.

"Is everything coming back to you?"

"Not everything by any means, but I was just recalling a woman who addressed me by that name. It was a memory from several years ago."

"So, you remember that. Anything else? She looked at him pointedly."

He had no answer for her.

"It's obvious you're a soldier for the Confederate Army.

Do you know what company you are in or how you happened upon our land?"

He looked down at his clothes. Sure enough, he was wearing a uniform so she probably was correct on that account. But he didn't remember being a soldier, and it caused him to wonder if it was a time of war or peace. All the thinking was starting to give him a headache.

"I really can't remember." Feeling the top of his head and running his fingers through his matted hair, he felt a goose egg above his temple. "I'm not sure how, when, or where, but I think someone knocked the wits out of me."

"I heard gunfire not far from here yesterday. Were you part of that skirmish?"

"Your guess is as good as mine, young lady. Is the country at war?"

Brigid looked at him with one eyebrow raised.

"You really don't remember? I guess that hit you took was worse than I suspected." She bit her lip, obviously pondering what to do with him.

"Could you possibly point me in the direction of a place where I could lie down for a couple of hours? Maybe when I wake up everything will come back to me. If there's fresh hay in the barn, I can sack out there."

Standing the hoe up on its head and gripping the handle, she tapped her right pointer finger on her chin. Dominic admired her surreptitiously as he awaited an answer.

"Let me think about this for a moment," she said before voicing her thoughts aloud. "You're a soldier in the Confederate Army and you're obviously wounded. It would be inhospitable to send you off to the barn to sleep with the livestock. If word got back to my father that I treated one of his soldiers poorly, he would be quite upset with me. Not only that, if the stable boy runs across you, you'll scare the child half to death and he's already spooked by everything as it is."

She glanced towards the house. "If I bring you into the house, I'll have to explain your presence to the household help and then, of course, my sisters will see you and no doubt tell our mother. I don't want to upset her — she's in a fragile state of mind lately as it is."

Dominic kept quiet as Brigid continued voicing her thoughts.

"You can't keep lying in the grass, the barn won't work, and if I send you off, Lord only knows where you'd end up."

She let out a sigh and put her free hand on her hip. "I suppose I could have you come in and rest for a bit."

Dominic's face brightened at the prospect of being the guest of such a lovely hostess.

"In the meantime, I will send one of the men to town. Maybe Father Barron would be willing to put you up for a few nights until you regain your senses."

"There's no need to bother a priest, Miss McGinnis," Dominic said hastily. "Let's just do this – find me a spot in an empty room and let me sleep for a few hours. Keep the door shut and chances are no one will run across me. By then I should be thinking clearly and can make my way back to wherever I'm supposed to be."

After a moment of hesitation, Brigid said, "That seems reasonable."

Setting the hoe down, she held out her hand to Dominic to help him up. The girl may not have been an angel, but her skin felt angel soft to the touch. He couldn't help but notice she wore no band on her left ring finger. Glancing at his own left hand, he noticed it was free of any adornment as well.

"I just hope to God you're not a murderous cur," Brigid

said as she put her full weight into tugging him to his feet.

"I hope to God I'm not either."

Chapter III

Brigid pointed the soldier in the direction of the privy towards the back of the yard. Her fingers tingled from his firm grasp on her hand when he was getting up from the ground. It was the first time she ever touched a man who wasn't related to her. She glanced at her hand front and back.

Shaking her head, she brought her thoughts to the present situation. With him being disposed for the moment, it would give her a chance to consider where to put him up once they went inside the house. She was grateful it was a Wednesday. If it had been a day earlier or later, Beulah would already be up kneading bread dough in the cook house and would have certainly noticed something going on in the yard as the woman traversed between the two buildings.

It was times like these when Brigid wished she were more decisive like her best friend, Amara McKirnan. The two of them met at Lucy Cobb the year it opened. Amara was a few months older than Brigid and was one grade ahead, so they didn't have any classes together. Fortunately, their paths crossed one fateful day at the school library.

Each of them was seeking asylum from their classmates. Brigid's father was a benefactor of the institute, so she was welcome in the circles of the upper crust, but she found she didn't fit in with those girls. She tried not to judge, but they were such a snippy bunch — it seemed their favorite pastime was gossiping and when they weren't talking about their fellow schoolmates, they were going on about boys, fashion and their much-anticipated debutante balls.

She tried to steer clear of their conversations because it was just as much a sin to listen to gossip as it was to spread it but, truth be told, she did enjoy talking about fashion. Brigid loved dressing in the latest styles. She did her best to be humble, since pride was one of the seven deadly sins, but she eagerly awaited the latest copy of *Godey's Magazine* and *Lady's Book* that came in the mail every month. She would devour it cover to cover and saved every issue. It was such an indulgence, especially during a time of war, since her father paid three dollars a year for the subscription. But she loved looking at pictures of bright, pretty dresses, fancy chapeaus and the newest hairstyles.

When it came to fashion, Brigid could hold court with any girl in her school — her parents made sure she represented the McGinnis family appropriately when she was out and about. Her mother brought her to the dressmaker twice a year to update her wardrobe and, with her trim figure, almost every dress style was flattering on her. Luckily, she was the oldest girl in their household, so all her clothes were new and tailored just for her. The dresses, gowns and riding habits were modified for her little sisters as they grew into them and fashions evolved.

Tilly accompanied Brigid to school to help her get dressed each morning, make her bed, wash her garments, and assist with her nighttime bedtime ritual. Her most vital task, in Brigid's eyes, was hairdressing. The girl was quite talented in that regard and could reproduce any hairstyle on Brigid they saw on the pages of *Godey's*.

As much time as the two spent together, most of their conversations centered on the marching orders for the day. Tilly was around Brigid's age and seemed nice enough, but she was unbearably timid. Mr. McGinnis wasn't keen about his children fraternizing with the household help, so in deference to him, Brigid didn't strike up any unnecessary conversations with her.

She did wonder what Tilly was like around the other handmaids who accompanied their mistresses to school. All the Negro help were housed in a separate building on the edge of the campus. Did the girls talk amongst themselves? On the days they weren't washing clothes, what did they do to stay busy? They certainly didn't spend their time reading like she did — Brigid's father told her Negroes didn't have the mental capacity to be educated.

As far as her classmates went, Brigid did not put nearly as much thought into the mores of society as they did. She looked the part, her speech was refined, and her manners were beyond reproach, but she didn't waste time speculating about her place in the social order. She'd leave that to her father.

When it came to boys, she seldom had any reason to interact with them. Before she transferred to the Lucy Cobb Institute, she attended Locust Grove Academy, the Catholic school on the grounds of The Church of the Purification of the Blessed Virgin Mary. She was one of a handful of girls who went to school there, and the females were segregated from the males. They didn't study together, they didn't eat together, and they certainly didn't play together.

The only time she had any contact with the boys was going to and from school. Her parents had instructed her to walk home with the girls from her class and not speak to any young men en route. She did her best to do as she was told.

It wasn't always an easy task because the boys would sometimes follow the girls as they headed home for the day. One particular young man was quite persistent. His name was Stewart Williams, and when he and Brigid were in fifth grade, she caught his interest. For some reason, he seemed to delight in picking on her. He and a couple friends, who, like him, lived outside of town on plantations, would follow behind the girls on horseback. Sometimes he'd hand the reigns of his horse over to his buddy, hoist himself out of the saddle and tag after Brigid on foot. He'd make a pest of himself by pulling her pigtails or blocking her way on the road as she walked.

Stewart's mother's side of the family was of the Maryland English and one of the original families that started their parish in 1792. The English had the church to themselves until families fleeing the French Revolution arrived in Georgia. Then the French slave-holding families came from Haiti, including Stewart's grandparents on his father's side after the Slave Revolt in 1798. The Germans became parishioners next and lastly the Irish, including Brigid's grandfather, entered the fold. Her grandparents emigrated from Ireland before the Great Hunger.

Word had it that one of Stewart's great-grandfathers had been murdered by a slave in the Haiti uprising. The slave was later executed, but his family's hatred towards Negroes had been fanned into flames over the years by Stewart's grandfather and father. The story tended to grow as time went on and those feelings were instilled in Stewart to a point where he seemed to think he had experienced what his great-grandfather had endured. Brigid heard that even at a young age, he dreamed of avenging his forefather.

By the time they were in sixth grade, Stewart was bigger and taller than all the eighth-grade boys. He still seemed to be enamored with Brigid even though she did nothing to encourage his attention. As petite as she was, there was no getting around him when he tried to impede her trek home, and she certainly couldn't outrun him. So when he insisted on halting her, she'd fold her hands together and say the Memorare out loud.

"Remember, O most gracious Virgin Mary, that never was it known that anyone who fled to thy protection, implored thy help, or sought thine intercession, was left unaided. Inspired by this confidence, I fly unto thee, O Virgin of virgins, my Mother. To thee do I come, before thee I stand, sinful and sorrowful. O Mother of the Word Incarnate, despise not my petitions, but in thy mercy, hear and answer me. Amen."

That was usually enough to make Stewart roll his eyes, say some snide comment about her trying to be the next Saint Brigid, and then signal the boys accompanying him to turn around and go their own way. It may have seemed dramatic, but Brigid really was looking for help from The Blessed Mother. Stewart frightened her, and it wasn't just because he was so much bigger than she was. She'd heard him bragging to his friends about doling out punishment to his father's slaves when they stepped out of line. He said his father even let him use a whip on their Negroes. The thought of hurting another human being sickened Brigid, and she couldn't shake that image out of her head any time she was forced to interact with the boy.

Unlike her classmates at Locust Grove Academy who were probably as afraid of Stewart as she was, Amara would have undoubtedly stood up for her. The girl had two older brothers, Michael and James, who teased her to no end, so she was accustomed to dealing with bothersome males. She would have figured out some clever way to make Stewart rue the day he ever set eyes on Brigid.

He probably wouldn't have known how to handle Amara. She was a feisty one, no doubt about it. Who would expect someone as pretty as her to have so much spirit? She had wavy auburn hair and sparkling aqua blue eyes — they were the color of the water in the Gulf of Mexico Brigid had visited once with her family. Stewart would be entranced by her looks before she took him down a notch or two.

She looked up to Amara, who was confident, decisive

and spoke her mind — albeit at times without thinking first.
But people overlooked that because she was witty and
charming. If only that spirited young lady were here right
now, she'd come up with a plan for dealing with the soldier.
But they hadn't seen each other since Amara left Lucy Cobb
after the war broke out. Amara's father couldn't afford to
have two daughters at the school at one time, and when her
stepsister Theresa came into the family, Mr. McKirnan felt
it was only proper the younger girl receive a formal
education since she never had that opportunity before.

A bird crying out overhead brought Brigid back to the
present time. She knew Amara wasn't going to appear out
of thin air and, as much as she hated being in this position,
she would have to figure things out for herself. She glanced
toward the sun. It was imperative to determine a place to
stash the soldier so no one would stumble across him.
Hopefully, a few solid hours of sleep would refurbish his
memory, and then he could determine his course of action
and she'd be off the hook. But time was running short before
the servants got up for the day, so she needed to come up
with an idea posthaste.

The dressing room next to her bedroom could work. If
she got her gown out and laid it on the bed before Tilly came
to dress her for the day, the servant would have no need to
enter the area. But if for some reason she did wander into
the alcove, Brigid would be beyond humiliated explaining a
man's presence in her chambers to a servant. As quiet as
Tilly was, Brigid couldn't imagine that anyone could keep a
story like that to themselves. She surmised that servants
gossiped with their peers just as much as the genteel folk
did.

Most every other room in the house was utilized in some
capacity throughout the day. The only door that remained
closed was her father's study – the children of the family

were forbidden from entering it.

Noticing Dominic walking towards her, Brigid needed to make a quick decision — one of her least favorite things to do. She was stuck between taking the chance of being seen as immoral — by having a man in her bedroom — or of disobeying her father. No matter which option she chose, it would mean she'd be facing Father Barron in the confessional on Saturday. She was there every week, so he knew her voice. At least this week she would have something worthwhile to confess — she tried so hard to be good that it took a lot of thinking to come up with new indiscretions to share with Father every seven days.

The proximity of the study, and the fact that her father wasn't home, made it the most logical choice. Plus, there would be less risk of running into somebody if they stayed on the first floor of the house. She just hoped her father would never find out.

With her mind made up, Brigid motioned to the man to follow her into the house. She held her pointer finger over her lips to signal him to remain quiet. They slowly walked up the creaky back steps of the house. Grabbing the handle of the woven wire door, Brigid winced when she heard the rusted hinges protesting as she pulled it towards her. She indicated to the soldier to move past her and pointed him toward the hall on the other end of the kitchen.

Going through the kitchen, Brigid grabbed a half loaf of bread that was sitting near the dry sink. The two of them shuffled quietly down the hall. When they came to the closed door on the right, Brigid turned the porcelain handle and pushed the wooden six-paneled door open. She let the man go in ahead of her. In passing, he brushed her shoulder with his arm. Brigid was taken aback by the strength emanating from him. Heat crept up her cheeks.

Taking a pause to gather her senses, she took a deep

breath and stepped into the room behind him. Once completely inside the space, she shut the door and pointed to the horsehair upholstered fainting sofa. Her father had installed the piece of furniture for her mother's comfort when she suffered bouts of female hysteria. The sofa also served as a place for Mrs. McGinnis to sit when she and her husband had household business to discuss in private — away from their children and the ever-vigilant servants.

"Your job is to get some sleep," whispered Brigid to Dominic as he arranged himself on the sofa. She knelt down near the piece of furniture and kept her voice low. Being face to face with him nearly took her breath away. "I won't be able to check on you until tonight when everyone has gone to bed. Once you have your wits about you again, we'll send you on your way."

"We?" inquired Dominic. "Would that be you and the Most Holy Father?"

"That would be the Royal We," Brigid shot back. "You may refer to me as Queen Brigid from this point out."

With that, she stood up.

"Yes, Your Royal Highness," Dominic said, with a chuckle. He gave her a slight bow.

"At least we didn't forget our sense of humor," she retorted in a hushed voice before departing from his presence.

Chapter IV

The fainting sofa was not overly large. Dominic had to bring his knees towards his chest so his feet wouldn't dangle off the end of the piece. He positioned himself on his left side to avoid putting pressure on the wounded right side of his skull.

What a strange predicament to be in, he thought. He pieced together what he gleaned while conversing with the young lady. Apparently, he was a soldier, the country was experiencing some type of conflict, he was injured — whether in battle or through an accident, he wasn't sure — and somehow ended up in the McGinnis family side yard.

He knew how to read in at least one language but could converse in two. If what little he recalled was true, his first name was Dominic and he lost his parents in a house fire. That fact should have made him sad but those folks were strangers to him now. He was in the military, so he was obviously of age. The person he saw in his mind escaping the fire was a young teen which meant the event must have happened several years ago.

Maybe he would never know what transpired before that time, but he hoped to recall what had happened to him since then. It may be unrealistic to have all the details, but he welcomed any tidbit that would come to mind.

Sleep was probably the best medicine to help his brain function as it should. Dominic shut his eyes and did his best to get comfortable in the small space he was provided. Once he settled in, Mr. Sandman took over and, with a few sprinkles of his magical dust, the dreams began.

He looked over the scene before him and realized there

was nothing he could do. The flames licked at the one-room house and when the entire dwelling was engulfed the whole structure collapsed. The house stood on a patch of clay with no vegetation close by, so the flames died down on their own.   When at last the flames flickered out completely, all that remained was a smoking mound of charred wood — the final resting place of his parents. Weary and heartbroken, all he could do was stare at the macabre scene.

The trance was broken by the sound of horses approaching. Two men galloped toward him at a breakneck pace. They skidded to a halt when they were within speaking range.

The first man directed a question at him before he swung himself down from his horse.

He didn't know what the man asked, so he gestured toward the rubble. "Mein Mutter and Mein Vater." His voice shook with sorrow.

The man furrowed his brow.   The other rider dismounted and the two walked towards the embers. They spoke quietly as they surveyed the scene.

After a few moments, they approached the boy again.

"Hank," said the first man, pointing at himself. "Luke," he said with a nod towards the second man. He then pointed at the youth.

"Dominic."

The other man held up ten fingers.

The boy held up all his fingers on both hands and then four fingers on his right hand.

"Hmmm," said Hank. He turned to the other rider and the two started a spirited conversation. After a minute or two, the younger man pulled a coin out of his pocket. Using *his thumb, he flipped the object spiraling into the air. At its peak, Hank called out a word. The coin fell to the dirt head side up.*

Hank didn't look happy with the result. Luke mounted his horse and, heaving a sigh, Hank followed suit. He extended a hand to the boy to pull him up behind him. The men jabbed their spurs into the horses' sides and the animals bolted away from the smoke and ash. The clicking as horseshoes hit the packed earth resounded in the air.

Dominic swam up from the depths of his subconscious. The noise he heard hadn't been in his dream. Shaking his head to get his bearings, he listened and heard a clicking sound again. He opened his eyes to pitch black. Running his hand over the surface beneath him, he recognized the horsehair sofa on which he lay down earlier.

Sitting up, he twisted from side to side to get the crick out of his back. Judging from how dark it was outside, he estimated he had been asleep for at least sixteen hours. As he rubbed his eyes to get the sleep out of them, his hand grazed the side of his head and he felt the dried blood in his hair and the contusion. His head throbbed, but not as much as it had the day before.

Bringing his mind back to the present, he considered the sound he just heard. It seemed to come from outside the window on the far side of the room. Instinct caused Dominic to drop to his hands and knees and crawl to the window situated two feet above the floor.

The sound was too deliberate to have been caused by an animal or the wind shifting something outside. *Who could be out there? People don't slink around at this time of night without good reason.*

Reaching the window, he positioned himself to the right of the opening and peered around the corner to see the property. Cloud cover made the night even darker than normal but, sure enough, he saw figures moving across the lawn.

Every few seconds another person would leave the cover of the house and hurry towards the barn on the far side of the yard. Dominic counted seven people in all. From the sizes, he figured two were grown men, and the rest were either women or teens. A couple of them looked to be bulkier, so they may have been adults holding younger children.

After a break of fifteen seconds, Dominic guessed all the people had vacated the house. The noise he had heard, as far as he could figure, was the sound of a latch being opened and closed. Perhaps the group had been sequestered in a root cellar or basement under the building.

Dominic tried to imagine why a group of people would be coming and going from this stately house in the middle of the night. *Was someone up to no good? Or perhaps they had some valid reason to be traveling under the cover of darkness.* While memories were starting to creep back to him, the state of affairs under which he now lived was still unknown to him.

Remembering the soldier's uniform he was wearing and Brigid's comments about gunfire being heard in the nearby area, Dominic wondered if the country he was living in was either waging war or under siege.

He had little time to dwell on that thought. Still looking outside from his vantage point, he saw movement again close to the house. By this time, the other fugitives had made it to the barn but, with his eyes adjusting to the darkness, he knew there was another person slowly slipping away.

The person was robed from head to toe in black, in what could have been perceived as a monk's gown. This one was definitely the tallest and broadest of the group. He stopped and looked back towards the house and the room Dominic was in.

Ducking his head, Dominic prayed he wasn't discovered. He held his breath for what seemed an eternity until he finally heard footsteps heading away from the house. Dominic released his breath and sunk to the floor. He was relieved that he hadn't been found out but perplexed by what he saw.

Somehow in his life, he must have had some sort of interaction with those people – whether it had been positive or negative, he wasn't sure. But he knew one thing: when the only part you could make out of a person's face in the dark was the whites of their eyes, it left little doubt. The person he saw — and perhaps every person he noticed slipping from the house — was a Negro.

Chapter V

Brigid gently turned the handle and pushed open the door to her father's study. By herself, she had managed to change from her nightgown back into the frock she wore earlier that day. She didn't want to alert Tilly, and more importantly, she refused to be seen again by the stranger wearing just her nightclothes. It took some doing, but she was able to make her hair presentable, even if she didn't have the preening skills her handmaid possessed.

Peering into the space, she could see the fainting sofa with its sculpted back and tufted upholstery. She expected it to be where it was when she last left the room, but she also expected to see the man where he was when she last left the room — reposing on the piece of furniture. She let out a gasp when she saw it was empty.

Good Lord. Her mind started to race. *How on earth did that soldier get misplaced?* Various scenarios went through her head as her eyes darted around the room, trying to make out the man's figure in the near-total darkness.

She looked towards the window, and as the shade was up, it afforded some visibility. That's when she saw the man hunkered down next to the portal with his right cheek pressed into the wall.

Slowly shutting the door behind her, she lightly clicked her fingers together to get the man's attention. Dominic spun around and sat with his back upright against the Gothic Revival wallpaper. His eyes widened.

Striding across the space, Brigid dropped to her knees next to Dominic.

"What in heaven's name are you doing?" asked Brigid in

a frantic whisper.

"*Nichts*," said Dominic.

She looked at him intently.

"Nothing," Dominic repeated.

"Let me rephrase that question. Why was your face plastered to my father's study wall when I walked in?"

After a beat, Dominic replied. "Just enjoying the cool air," he said nonchalantly.

"*Really...*" Something fishy was going on here. "You weren't able to imbibe the cool air from your position on the sofa?" Brigid asked looking at him askance.

"The closer a person gets to the source, the easier it is to take in, wouldn't you agree?"

She furrowed her eyebrows.

"Was there, perhaps, something you were looking for in the yard?" she inquired.

Brigid started to stand up to go look for herself, but Dominic pulled the sleeve of her gown so sharply she tumbled back and nearly landed on his lap. He caught her in time to break the fall.

Cheeks blazing from being in close proximity to such a good-looking man, she disentangled herself from his grasp and backed away.

"Are you addled as well as memory impaired?" she asked, putting more distance between the two of them. He had been gentle with her, but she sensed he was a man of great strength. Her father was a powerful man, as far as wielding authority, but not powerful physically like the young man before her. It was unnerving.

The soldier didn't answer. After taking a prolonged glance out the window, he got up stiffly and walked to the sofa. He settled himself on the far end. Brigid followed suit and sat on the other end, putting as much space between the two of them as she could without slipping to the floor.

Smoothing her dress, she shifted her thoughts back to where she abandoned them upon first entering the room.

"Mister Dominic, I trust you had an adequate amount of sleep or you probably wouldn't have been wandering about when I walked in." She paused and gave him a sideways glance, taking a quick moment to admire his profile. "Have you by chance started to piece together your life and how you came to be on our property yesterday?"

"Yes and no," replied Dominic.

"Explain yourself, if you please."

"Yes, memories of my childhood came to mind in my slumber. But they were less than fortunate ones. I believe I lost my parents when I was a teen."

Even though she was trying to maintain a neutral posture in front of the stranger, she couldn't keep the frown from her face. Unbidden, the thought of *That Day* came to mind.

"I'm so sorry to hear that," she said instinctively. Immediately, by rote, she launched into the Requiem Eternam — the prayer for the eternal rest of their souls. "*Requiem eternam, Domine. Et lux perpetua luceat ei. Requiescat in pace.* Amen."

Dominic gave her a blank look.

"You're not Catholic then," Brigid conjectured.

"If that's what Catholics speak, then probably not." He looked perplexed. "But when I glanced again at the book I had on my person, the cover page said it was a Roman Catholic Bible, so maybe I am. But I have no idea what you just said," he replied.

"It's Latin. 'Eternal rest, grant unto them, O Lord. And

let perpetual light shine upon them. May they rest in peace. Amen.'"

"The only word I understood the first time you said it was 'Amen,'" Dominic admitted.

Brigid tamped down the smile that threatened to cross her face before she continued.

"You said you can recall parts of your childhood. Do you have memories of attending Mass? Mass is celebrated in Latin. We learned it in school as well."

"At this point, I have no recollection of much of anything other than the farm I lived on with my parents. I can't tell you if I attended Mass or even school for that matter."

That wasn't the answer for which Brigid looked. She was hoping to get the matter of his circumstances resolved promptly, but it didn't look like it would be as simple of a task as she would have liked. Since her father was out of town and her mother was not up to handling anything other than getting herself through another day, Brigid would need to find someone else to go to for counsel.

With her dearest friend living in Atlanta and no McGinnis relation close by, there was only one other person in whom she could confide. She would go to morning Mass and talk to Father Barron in private afterward. Even outside the confines of the confessional, she felt secure he would keep the matter private and help her discern the best course of action for dealing with the soldier.

In the meantime, she'd have to see to Dominic's comfort if he was to be their guest for at least another day. As risky as it could be for him to leave the study, he would need to use the convenience and have something to eat and drink.

So the two of them left the room and headed to the rear of the house. When Dominic slipped out the back door, Brigid walked into the pantry and grabbed some freshly canned peaches, another loaf of bread, a fork, two starched cloth napkins, a drinking glass, and a pitcher of water that had been drawn from the well earlier in the evening.

She balanced the items in her hands and waited for Dominic to return. Once he came back through the door she motioned with her head towards the study. When they were securely in the room, she closed the heavy door behind them with her slippered foot.

One at a time, she set the objects on her father's desk. There would be no reason for her to stay while he ate, but she felt compelled to attend to the wound on his head before she went back upstairs.

With a wave of her hand, she instructed him to sit on the sofa. Grabbing one of the napkins off the desk, she doused it with water from the copper pitcher and timidly approached Dominic with the two items. She knelt down, placed the pitcher on the floor, and turned squarely towards him.

Brigid took a deep breath and began lightly running the fingers on her right hand through Dominic's hair to find the edge of the wound. His hair was even thicker than hers and had a coarse texture. She was tempted to linger a bit, but it felt as though Dominic was shivering. She needed to be quick about her ministrations in case he was developing a fever.

It made her jittery being so close to him, but this needed to be done. Finding her mark, she then took the pointer finger of her left hand and gently tilted his chin back. The stubble of his beard scratched her fingertip. At that moment, she looked directly into his eyes, and her heart fluttered. She had never seen eyes so enticing — they were such a dark blue that it could almost be said they were purple and they were outlined with even darker eyelashes. This time she was the one shivering. *Maybe something's going around.*

As she brought the napkin to his temple, she took a deep breath willing herself not to get woozy at the sight of the blood. She tried to imagine she was washing mud out of his hair, just like she did for her little sisters after they romped outside on a rainy day. She soon came to realize that crusted blood didn't dissolve as easily as mud did. Brigid needed to rewet the napkin several times and, as much as she wanted to be gentle, she had to use some force to scrub the area clean.

Dominic winced from the vigorous scouring but made no sound. When Brigid was finally satisfied with her work and folded up the cloth, he visibly relaxed.

"If the debutante role doesn't work out for you, you could make yourself a career in the torturing business," he jested.

A scowl crossed her face. She wasn't sure if she was more offended by being accused of having a sadistic nature or by his implication she was a spoiled young lady.

"If you didn't like the way I was doing it, you certainly could have taken over the task yourself," she grumbled. "In any case, I have no intentions of becoming an inquisitor or joining the ranks of Georgian high society," Brigid said smugly. "I'm actually discerning the religious life."

"When you say 'discerning the religious life,' do you mean you're thinking of becoming a nun?" Dominic looked at her incredulously.

"Of course, what else would I mean?"

"Why?"

That was actually a very good question and one she had asked herself. Thinking back, the answer was somewhat complicated.

The previous May, after Brigid completed eleventh grade at the Lucy Cobb Institute, her father sat her down to present options for her life after graduation. What it boiled down to was she could either prepare to enter formal society and begin the vetting process to find an eligible husband or, since she was bright, she could continue her studies.

Like any girl her age, Brigid would have loved to enter society and be the toast of the town. However, with the state their country was in, there were almost no suitable bachelors available. Even if they hadn't been in the midst of a war, Brigid wasn't sure how her entrance into society would have been met. There were so many pretty girls her age, she felt quite plain in comparison to them.

Times being what they were, going on for more schooling seemed to be the most sensible selection for her. If she had been male and the country wasn't in conflict, the logical choice would be to apply to Mr. McGinnis' alma mater Harvard University and take up the study of banking.

As a female, however, the courses of study available were limited. She certainly had the intelligence to pursue a degree in nursing or education, but neither of those fields appealed to her. The sight of blood nauseated her, and she didn't know if she was cut out to be a teacher.

Under the current circumstances, finding a school would be tricky. There were a handful of colleges in the United States that accepted female students; however, they were all in Union states. Studying abroad sounded intriguing, but the southern ports were blockaded by the Union Army.

The only other choice was continuing her education through the Church. That was a decision not to be made lightly because, in order to do that, she would need to join a religious order. Several were scattered throughout the South and even some in states as distant as California, which would keep her far from the hostilities.

Brigid had a deep devotion to her faith, but she wasn't sure if it was the right vocation for her. From her understanding, the Holy Spirit called people to join the religious life. As hard as she tried to listen for that voice inviting her to become a bride of Christ, she hadn't heard it yet.

For more than a year, Brigid delayed making a decision, hoping the war would end by the time she graduated. Unfortunately, things had gotten worse for the South in the last twelve months. There was no end to the conflict in sight.

With no discernible sign, entering the convent was probably the most sensible choice. She felt she had the temperament for that sacred endeavor, and if it wasn't her calling, she would leave after the postulancy period was complete.

After she voiced her thoughts to her father, Mr. McGinnis made it his mission to find the most prestigious religious institution in which to enroll his daughter. He mailed letters to the top religious orders on his list. It would take time to gather the information he needed, so Brigid had a few months to get in the proper frame of mind for this new endeavor.

If Brigid had her druthers, she would study finance with the sisters, so she could run a religious order. Like her father, she had a talent with numbers and was adept at keeping things running properly, as was evidenced by how efficiently she ran the household in her mother's stead. Not that her mother acknowledged her contributions. The woman gave her as much deference as any one of their servants. But the idea of studying finance was neither here nor there — even though religious orders were populated by women, they were still run by men.

Brigid did look forward to going back to school — she had a love for learning. Her future education would be filtered through Church doctrine, which was fine with her; she was determined to soak in as much as she could.

Advancing one's education was always a worthwhile endeavor, even if it turned out she never stepped foot in a classroom or infirmity or had children of her own to teach.

Not wanting to bore the poor man to death, Brigid attempted to give him a condensed version of her story. For some reason, he seemed intrigued and encouraged her to expound on her narrative. It was somewhat uncomfortable at first going on and on about herself, but, with his encouragement, she told him the entire tale — less the parts that painted her in a less-than-flattering light.

When she finished, she checked to see Dominic's reaction. "Your life seems very well-thought-out." His eyes shifted to the left as though he was considering her words. "Maybe it's just me, but as rational as it sounds, I have a hard time picturing you in a habit singing the Angelus and wiling away the hours on your knees praying."

While she may have had similar thoughts herself over the last several months, Brigid still bristled. She stood up, arms akimbo. "For a person who can't remember a darned thing about himself, you certainly seem like quite the know-it-all. What exactly do you mean by that comment?"

He gave her a rakish smile. "You would be more temptation than even the most pious reverend could withstand, *Schatzie*. Those men may be priests, but they aren't saints."

Her jaw dropped open. *How dare he say something so scandalous!* Any other woman would have slapped a man across the face for being so impertinent, but she could not bring herself to do such a thing. Rather, she chose the next best option. She balled up the stiff napkin that was still in her hand and threw it at his head. He easily ducked out of the way.

That infuriated her even more. She crossed her arms

over her chest. He may be the most handsome male she ever set eyes on, but his attitude was insufferable. That man needed to go back from whence he came.

"Twenty-four hours. That's it. You are leaving these premises come hell or high water."

Dominic couldn't help it. He gave her a sharp salute and responded, "Yes, *Mein Kapitän*."

Stamping her foot soundlessly, Brigid whirled around and stalked towards the door.

"I'll show you who's captain."

Chapter VI

If it didn't hurt his head so much, Dominic would have laughed out loud from his encounter with Brigid. *She looks demure enough, but she has some fire in her. She just needs the right person to bring it out.*

While he would more than relish that opportunity, the chance of them spending much more time together was unlikely. Brigid obviously was concocting some arrangement since she made it more than clear that she was giving him the boot before sunrise the next morning.

In the meantime, he was determined to wring his brain and see if he could squeeze any more information out of it. Thanks to the chit's tender care, his headache was in full force again. Maybe if he had something to drink and eat he'd feel better.

He gulped down his fill of water, unscrewed the metal lid from the quart jar, and started digging peach halves out of the glass container. Between each piece of fruit, he ripped off chunks of bread and eagerly devoured them. After he swallowed the last drop of peach juice from the jar, he was satiated and weariness overtook him.

If sleep was the magical elixir that brought his memory back, he would be more than happy to indulge in it, something he sensed was a luxury for him. Settling back into position on the sofa, he yawned deeply and in the blink of an eye, was out again.

After a ten-minute ride, the two men went their separate ways. Hank turned his horse toward a modest ranch house set amongst acres of wheat. As they approached, the door swung open. A woman stepped out onto the wooden porch.

She placed her hands on her hips as the two drew near. A scowl crossed her face after they dismounted. She ground out a question to Hank.

With an apologetic tone, he gave her a lengthy answer. After he said his piece, he placed his hands on the boy's shoulders and urged him to step closer to the lady.

"Charity," he said, indicating the woman.

The female peered at him skeptically. Not knowing what else to do, the young man greeted the woman. "Wie gehts, Frau Charity."

His words incensed her. She exploded in a tirade. The boy recognized the word 'kraut,' which was hurled in his direction several times. The derogatory term led him to believe she held some animosity towards Germans.

After winding down, the woman whirled around and crossed back over the threshold of the house. She slammed the door behind her.

Swiveling his head to the left to gauge Hank's reaction, he noticed two sets of eyes peering at him from the side of the house. A pair of boys scurried towards him and the man. They had a striking resemblance to Hank. While they were both taller than he was, Dominic guessed the one was his elder by a year or so and the other one was slightly younger than him.

The two brothers turned toward each other and shared a knowing look. Dominic didn't know what they were thinking, but he had a feeling it wasn't going to bode well for him.

That thought was quite prophetic as Hank's sons Billy and Danny found great satisfaction making Dominic's life unbearable. Begrudgingly, their mother had acquiesced and allowed him to stay on the farm — with the condition that he sleep in the barn and earn his keep. What was intended to be a stay of a few weeks turned out to be several months. During that time, the brothers managed to force him to do twice his share of work, so they could play hooky and wander off to the swimming hole on hot summer afternoons or to the creek to fish. If chores didn't get done on the farm, the finger of blame always pointed at him.

While he was grateful to Hank for taking him in, he resented the rest of his kin. It irked him to be treated like a slave when he knew he contributed greatly towards the farm. Everyone else's life got easier once he arrived, except his.

To add insult to injury — or more like injury to insult — Hank got the brilliant idea to teach his boys how to box. It was a survival skill he honed growing up on the streets of New York City after he arrived in America as a youngster. Billy and Danny used their newfound skills on their rival, who, they determined, was an ideal punching bag. At first, he didn't have the strength or the skills to defend himself, but in time he developed the speed to dodge their jabs. As he grew more muscular working sunup to sundown sowing and harvesting crops and taking care of the animals, he built up the strength to fight back.

He eventually had the power to knock either of them on their backsides but always held himself in check, which wasn't easy because he had a short fuse, which had already gotten him into trouble. But Hank had the attitude that boys will be boys, so he never stepped in when the sparring started. However, if the young man ever were to let loose, which he was tempted to do on many an occasion, there would be hell to pay — maybe not from Hank but most certainly from his wife.

Charity never could stand the sight of him. He wasn't sure why because he treated her as respectfully as he had

his own mother. But, unlike her sons, who could do no
wrong in her eyes, he could do no right. When he felt
comfortable enough to do so, he broached the topic with
Hank. The man attributed his wife's behavior to her
Austrian heritage.

It was a flimsy excuse to the boy. Regardless, the
woman nurtured a constant state of tension between the
two of them. Frau Charity seemed to look for moments to
corner him. When he needed to draw water from the well,
he waited until she was out of sight. If she spied him, it
would, by chance, be the exact moment she needed water
as well. She'd come up behind him bearing whatever tool
was close at hand — be it a rug beater or a broom — and
apply it to his backside to get him out of her way. For a
small woman, she had a solid hook shot. No wonder Hank
seemed skittish around her — maybe she should have been
the one teaching their sons to box.

Living on the farm allowed him to hone his English
skills — it was essential so he could follow orders. But even
that got him in trouble. One time the boys went through the
ruse of teaching him some new words. They told him it
would impress their mother if he used proper English when
he got his chow. Per the boys' instructions, he practiced
saying, "Thank you for this fabulous meal," over and over.
That evening when he stepped inside the house and was
handed his dinner plate, he enunciated each word as he
thanked his hostess for the food.

Rather than looking pleased, Charity slapped the tin
plate out of his hand, took hold of him by the ear and
dragged him to the dry sink. She grabbed the bar of lye
soap, shoved it into his mouth, and held it there until his
eyes watered so badly, it looked like he was crying.

The only real crying going on in the house came from
Danny and Billy who laughed so hard that tears ran down

their cheeks. Charity finally pulled the bar of soap out of his mouth, kicked him squarely on the rear end with her work boot, and sent him out to the barn with no supper. She told him boys who talked filth didn't deserve to eat.

It took a while before Dominic figured out what had been so offensive about what he had said to Frau Charity. After getting a better grasp on the English language, he was mortified to discover the word he used to describe the meal started with the same first letter but was considerably less civilized than the word fabulous.

If he had been anywhere in the vicinity of Billy and Danny when he had that realization, he would have finally beat the snot out of them, like they deserved. Lucky for them, the chances of ever crossing paths with either of them again was slim. And after close to a year working his tail off on the farm, he turned sixteen and set off on his own to see if he could hire himself out for wages — rather than scraps of food and a pile of hay on which he could lay his head.

Chapter VII

Even though Brigid had been in her bedroom for nearly an hour, she could not settle down and fall asleep. After a while, she gave up and got out of bed, put her dressing gown back on and settled into the Empire chair.

She felt ashamed for losing her temper with Dominic. The poor man was obviously still not thinking clearly after the blow to his head. It was so unlike her to talk in such a snippety fashion. Now that she thought of it, Dominic surely must consider her unbearably rude.

Her classmates at Locust Grove Academy would have certainly been surprised if they had witnessed that encounter — especially Stewart. The pestering he did to her in fifth and sixth grade turned to taunting by the time they were in seventh grade. Maybe he was incensed because she didn't give him the time of day when most of the other girls thought he was a bang-up guy.

That year he decided he would be clever and instead of addressing her by her given name, he started calling her 'Field Mouse.' At first, Brigid thought it was fun-natured joking, but she quickly came to the realization that the joke was at her expense. He'd point out her mousey manners, her mousey brown hair, and her mouse-like features. Soon he had the other boys following suit.

Brigid did whatever she could to stay out of Stewart's way. Every encounter with him gave her a stomachache that would last all evening and into the night.

On school mornings, Brigid could easily avoid him because she held fast to the adage that being on time meant arriving ten minutes early for any given appointment. So she was safely ensconced in the building with her female classmates before he pulled up at breakneck speed on his horse just as the bell was being rung for the start of the school day.

Walking home from school was a different story. If Stewart was bound and determined to detain her, there was little she could do about it. None of her classmates stood up for her — Brigid presumed no one wanted to take her place as the whipping boy and be Stewart's next target. It was out of the question to say anything to the sisters as she was too embarrassed to bring up the topic. She couldn't tell her parents because she was not supposed to be talking to boys, so she would have been blamed for bringing this on herself.

This went on for two years, and Brigid wasn't sure how much more she could take. She was completely losing confidence in herself and dreaded going to school. Then came one of the best days in her life — the summer after eighth grade Mr. McGinnis told Brigid he had enrolled her at the Lucy Cobb Institute, and she would start school there when the campus buildings were complete.

Knowing relief was in sight, Brigid was better able to withstand the barbs Stewart threw her way. She counted down the weeks until she would transfer to her new school. When the last day at Locust Grove Academy finally arrived, it felt like the weight of the world had been lifted from her shoulders. She said goodbye to the girls in her class with little fanfare — she was still a bit resentful that they did not come to her defense when Stewart was so mean to her.

As for Stewart, she took one last glance over her shoulder at him as she left the school grounds. A mixture of feelings welled up inside her. It would be wicked to say she hated him, but she disliked him very, very much. She did feel a bit sorry for him because people said he was the target of brutality himself at the hands of his father. Brigid had seen bruises scattered across his arms and face through the years. She wondered if they had been inflicted on him as punishment.

But that didn't give him license to take anything out on her. She didn't wish harm to any human being, but if Stewart fell off the face of the planet one day and she never saw him again, she would feel no remorse. *One could only hope.*

It really didn't matter anyhow. Stewart lived miles outside of town and the only time she saw him was at church – and he wouldn't dare accost her there. Not that he graced the building with his presence that often. His parents were there every week as would be anyone of their social status, but his visits were few and far between. When he was in grade school he made no secret of the fact that he had no use for church. Brigid could remember seeing him slip outside during the middle of Mass on a number of occasions probably to meet up with his friends so they could smoke hand-rolled cigars behind the school house.

During the years Brigid attended the Lucy Cobb Institute, she did see Stewart at the Church of the Purification of the Blessed Virgin Mary a few times but gave him a wide berth because he still caused her to tense up when he was in her vicinity. She even avoided eye contact with him — if he caught her glancing in his direction, he'd scrunch up his face in what he undoubtedly determined was the look of a field mouse and mouth the words, "Squeak, squeak." Even that was enough to ruin her day.

Brigid shook her head to clear her thoughts of Stewart. It was much more intriguing to think of the man holed up in her father's study. After putting more thought into the matter, she was certain the remarks he made were contrary to his character. She didn't know much about him, but she was sure he was the complete opposite of that brute Stewart. Dominic's good looks put Stewart's to shame. Plus, he was undeniably smart, witty, and hard-working, judging by his muscular build. In essence, he was everything Brigid wanted in a man. *Me and every other girl*, she thought as a sigh escaped her lips. But Dominic would be hers only in her dreams. The man surely must be taken by now — and undoubtedly it would be by a young lady much more desirable than her.

Chapter VIII

The man in question was still wrapped up in his own dreams and trying to untangle the threads woven to create the fabric of his life.

The closest town was Tonica, so he made it his goal to set off in that direction. If he had the ability to correspond in English he would have left a note on the doorframe saying he was leaving, but since he wasn't capable of doing that, he decided he needed to confide in Hank before he left.

The man had treated him decently. Even if his boys were miscreants and his wife was the devil incarnate, Dominic would always be grateful to Hank for taking him in. He actually pitied him because long after he was gone, Hank would still have to deal with his family. Of course, someday the boys would be on their own, but the man had spoken wedding vows with that shrew, so he was tied to her for life.

That realization convinced Dominic he would be very particular when it came time to ask a young lady for her hand in marriage. He'd want to know her in good times and bad before he committed to any vows.

Leaving the farm went smoothly, since he made his departure before the rooster even started warming up his vocal chords for the day. Dominic walked off with a stick over his shoulder that had an oversized bandana tied to the end. The weather was warm, but he had cool weather gear tied up in the bundle. Frau Charity would have been incensed seeing him leave with any of their possessions, but the coat was a hand-me-down from Danny, so they had no use for it anymore unless they intended to make rags out of it.

Thus began months of living the life of a nomad. He went from property to property, offering his service in fields and on ranches, laboring wherever he could to earn money. He developed empathy for the Negroes — like them, he worked so hard for so little. At the rate he was going, it would take him ten years to scrape enough money together to get his own place. If that wasn't bad enough, sometimes he'd work for a farmer for weeks and be cheated out of his pay. When they were done with his services, he'd be run off the property at gunpoint and could do nothing to get what was owed to him.

He endured that first winter with difficulty. The weather that year in Illinois was colder than anything he had ever lived through. Working kept him relatively warm, but on the days he couldn't find gainful employment, he had to steal away into barns and use the warmth from the animals to keep from freezing. He resorted to eating slop and hay to put a dent in the empty hole in his belly.

As much as he hated to do it, he'd even gotten so low that he had broken into a few churches to escape the cold. Pews were hard, but they gave him a place to lay his head. However, no matter how hungry he was, Dominic couldn't bring himself to partake of the provisions in the sacristy. They weren't consecrated, so the food was still bread and wine, not the body and blood of Christ, but he didn't want to anger God and suffer His wrath. He was doing his best to find his way in the world and he wanted to be in good standing with God.

The following summer, he discovered that he was still good with God. After months of praying for a better situation, he happened upon a ranch owned by Jacob Murphy and his wife Mary Louise, a young couple who were in the family way. Their child was due to arrive that fall. Mary Louise had her hands full raising her younger brothers and sisters since their mother had passed away the year before. Jacob was more than happy to bring on extra help as their operation had grown considerably since its inception two years earlier.

Dominic was immediately welcomed into their home. He was given a room to share with the boys: Nathan, David and Stephen. The most difficult task he faced at first was keeping the girls' names straight. Ruth, Anne, Adele and Frances had only five years between them from oldest to youngest. With their ebony hair, fair skin and blue-gray eyes, they looked uncannily similar to each other.

It turned out that Nathan was less than a year younger than Dominic and the two hit it off immediately. With similar levels of intellectual capacity and work ethic and the same sense of humor, they could have been brothers. In fact, Dominic was probably closer in nature to Nathan than even David and Stephen were.

Looks-wise, the two were opposites. Nathan was tall, lean, fair-skinned most of the year, and had the same color eyes and wavy dark hair that his sisters had. Dominic, on the other hand, was just above average height, had a stocky build, straight dark brown hair, and eyes his mother called "violett." Having eyes the shade of a flower sounded sissy to Dominic — he considered himself to be blue-eyed.

Physically, both young men had been blessed with muscular physiques and after all the time they spent working the land, the two were both strong as oxen. They developed a keen sense of competition with each other. If it wasn't a test of brawn — to see who could put the most bales of hay in the barn loft in the shortest amount of time or who could beat the other in a game of wrist wrestling — then it was a test of brains, as almost daily they tried to outwit each other over a game of checkers.

Providence may have brought them together, but their enterprising spirit and sense of adventure bonded them and sent them off on the journey of a lifetime. They grew so close that each one would have gladly given his life for the other one. As time unfolded, one of them nearly did.

Chapter IX

Seeing that the study had been left undisturbed the previous day, Brigid felt confident that she could leave the house that morning without fear of Dominic being discovered by anyone. After eating a breakfast of scrambled eggs and dry toast, she asked the kitchen girl to tell the footman to bring the horse and buggy up from the barn. She then went up to her bedroom to get her spoon bonnet. Once downstairs again, she stopped in front of the oval looking-glass hung on the wall with a heavy velvet ribbon. With a critical eye, she surveyed herself, then adjusted the headpiece. She put two hat pins in to secure it to her head and was ready to go.

Agnes and Martha caught her primping in the mirror and knew she was headed somewhere. They demanded to know where Brigid was going. Not wanting to be dishonest, she said she was riding into town but didn't elaborate on her plans. She intended to see Father Barron and since the girls were both notorious for tattling, she didn't want them to know because they would be blabbing to their mama.

"Please, Brigid, take us with you," pleaded Agnes. "We'll be good."

Martha joined in. "Please. It's so boring staying home every day. We've no one to play with and Mother won't let us leave the yard to go exploring."

"One week out of school and you're already bored," exclaimed Brigid. "Maybe we can find some chores for you to do around the house. I'm sure they could use help in the kitchen."

Both girls shook their heads vigorously in the negative,

their dark brown ringlets dancing back and forth as they did. Their little lower lips stuck out as they put on their best pouty faces. It pained Brigid to see them unhappy so she resorted to bribery.

"I would love to have both of you accompany me, but Jeremiah is only pulling up the gig. There's not room for all of us in there. How about I bring you each a piece of stick candy from town?"

That brought the smiles back to their faces. They started going through the flavors available. Between them, they were able to recall all nine varieties the grocer carried — peppermint, rose, clove, lemon, wintergreen, horehound, lavender, birch and orange. Then the deciding time came. After agonizing over the decision for a minute, Agnes chose horehound — she loved the combination of mint and black licorice. Martha still couldn't make up her mind.

By this time Jeremiah had pulled up to the front of the house. Knowing how long it could take her to decide, Brigid told Martha she would surprise her with whatever flavor looked tastiest that day. Martha loved surprises, so she was amenable to that offer.

After Brigid went outside, Jeremiah assisted her into the buggy. Politely thanking him, the thought struck her that even though he was considerably older than her father's manservant, Mr. Mason, everyone addressed him by his first name. Come to think of it, all the servants were addressed by their first names, except Mr. Mason.

The man traveled with Brigid's father back and forth between Dallas and Richmond, seldom leaving his side. When the two men were in Dallas, Mr. Mason had a private residence on the third floor of their house, adjacent to the two rooms shared by the other house servants.

He was quite the distinguished gentleman. His posture,

manners and speech were impeccable. The way he carried himself a person could think *he* was the business owner and master of the house. While he kept his thoughts to himself, Brigid knew he was cognizant of most everything that went on in their household. His brown eyes seemed to take it all in, yet his visage seldom changed. The few words he did utter were spoken with authority.

Mr. Mason, like the rest of the staff, was a free black under the employ of the McGinnis family. Other than Beulah, who ruled the roost in the kitchen, no other servant had the confident demeanor of the manservant. The lower-ranking servants scuttled about the house, doing as they were told and keeping their eyes downcast as they listened to orders. The children's nurse was kind and gentle towards them but seemed to fear Mr. and Mrs. McGinnis, which Brigid thought odd. She attributed that to the woman's nervous disposition.

Mr. McGinnis was not morally opposed to slavery but did admit to being leery of slave uprisings. While it would be unusual for such a thing to happen in the city, he knew it was a possibility. He was old enough to remember the Nat Turner Rebellion in 1831.

When the War Between the States broke out, it appeared he had made a prudent decision to staff his house with free blacks. Everyone remained in his employ, whereas other households lost a number of house slaves, as they found the upheaval an ideal opportunity to escape their masters.

Brigid dismissed the unsavory thought of the whole slave issue. She turned in her seat to wave to the girls, who were standing in front of the parlor window, and then instructed Jeremiah to take her to the town square. She wanted to check the notices nailed to the post in front of her father's business. One of the employees at the bank had the duty of updating the lists of the local dead and injured servicemen as word arrived in town each week.

As macabre as it seemed, Brigid couldn't help herself and had to look the lists over every time she was in town. She checked to see if any classmates from Locust Grove Academy or any of the young men from their parish were on the list. It saddened her to see the names of people she knew listed among the casualties. But living in a community as small as theirs, it was inevitable that would happen. If she knew the family of the deceased, she would make a point of sending a note of condolence to the next of kin. It was the least she could do.

After she finished looking at the notices, she would get the sweets for the girls from the dry goods store and then meet with Father Barron. The footman would make no mention of the trip to her family. Like the other servants, Jeremiah kept his thoughts to himself while in the vicinity of whites. She imagined there would be talk amongst the household staff about Miz Brigid seeing the clergyman in the middle of the week. There wasn't much she could do about that — even if she was their employer, she couldn't forbid them from gossiping. It was just human nature no matter what color a person's skin was.

Gossiping was universal, undoubtedly. Brigid never forgot the lesson she learned about it from Sister Francis Ann when she was in third grade. Sister asked them to imagine they had a pillow filled with feathers and the students climbed to the top of a hill and then slit the pillow open and shook it. Feathers would be caught in the wind and fly everywhere. When she asked them if they would be able to get all the feathers back after they had been shaken free from the pillow, they all agreed it would be impossible. "That's how it is with gossip," she cautioned them. "Every time you gossip, it's like shaking that pillow and letting the feathers fly. Even if you find out later that what you said wasn't true, no matter how hard you try, you can never get those words back."

Reminiscing about her early years in school kept her mind occupied during the ten-minute jaunt into town. The brightly shining sun made Brigid glad she was conducting her errands in the morning before it got too warm. When they arrived on the square, the footman climbed down from his seat and helped her out of the conveyance. Brigid snapped open her parasol. It wasn't overly large, but it would help shade the sun from her eyes. Her bonnet, with the fashionable short brim, was purely ornamental.

She crossed the square to get to the wooden stand. There were only a few people milling around the postings. Out of respect, she stood back and waited for a minute as a couple went through each name one by one. The elderly lady dabbed her eyes with a handkerchief which, in all likelihood, indicated that she knew someone whose name was on the list. With the aid of a carved wooden cane, she turned and hobbled away, leaning on the arm of an older gentleman whom Brigid surmised was her husband.

Once the couple left, the path was clear for Brigid to get close enough to read the notices. Looking over the sheet, she was relieved to see just three new names added to the list of injured and no new names under the death column. Brigid recalled the gunfire she heard the other night. *Perhaps that's when those unfortunate men were hurt.*

Glancing down the list a little further, she saw another heading titled Missing in Action. There were several names in that column. Looking them over quickly, a name caught her eye. Corporal Dominic Warner, 53rd Tennessee Infantry.

Brigid's heart started to race. *Could that be the Dominic who had stumbled into their yard?* Recalling the overcoat he had on when she found him, she could picture the two blue chevrons sewed to each of its sleeves. She knew privates had one chevron. Would two chevrons indicate the rank of corporal?

The name Dominic wasn't that common, and if that was his rank, it would seem most probable they were one and the same man. If that was the case, then she needed to decide what to do with Corporal Warner. Knowing his regiment was a plus, but chances were the 53rd Tennessee was long gone in their pursuit to push the Union troops out of Georgia.

Returning a soldier suffering from memory loss to the battlefield could prove to be fatal for the man. Brigid would never be able to live with herself if she did such a thing to him. She was grateful she could talk this through with Father Barron. He was probably close to fifty — a man that advanced in age would certainly have wisdom to share and could help her in this dilemma.

With that positive note in mind, she strode back to the gig. When she got there, she informed Jeremiah that he could remain where he was parked, since he had a shady spot, and she would walk to the corner where the mercantile was located. The look he gave her let her know he wasn't comfortable with that idea, but she assured him she would be within his range of sight, and if anything was amiss, he could come to her assistance in no time.

That may have been an overstatement because Jeremiah was older than the hills and she doubted he could get anywhere in 'no time.' But it was such a lovely day, Brigid desired to walk at her own pace. Having been cooped up in the house since Dominic arrived, she wanted to enjoy some fresh air and brisk movement.

Tipping the parasol over her shoulder, Brigid stepped out in front of the buggy and, looking left to right for oncoming traffic, proceeded to cross the packed earthen street. She was glad they hadn't had any rain for a few days;

otherwise, the mud would have ruined her McKays. There was a shortage of shoes since the war started, so she was cautious to take care of the few pairs she had.

Once on the other side, she took two steps up to the boardwalk and headed towards the business she needed to visit. Glancing in the window of the butcher shop, a large turkey caught her eye. She hadn't seen a Tom that big in at least two years — she made a mental note to have the kitchen girl come back to town with Jeremiah later that day to purchase it, if it was still available.

She turned to continue her trek and nearly collided with a man who was coming her way on the boardwalk.

"Pardon me," she said instinctively.

The man stood stock still. Brigid pulled her parasol down so she could see why he wasn't stepping out of her way. Tilting her head back to see the man's visage, she recognized him, and the blood drained from her cheeks.

Good Lord, it was Stewart Williams. She hadn't seen him since the previous summer. It took an act of will for her not to make The Sign of the Cross.

"Well, look here, if it isn't Saint Brigid of the Church of the Purification of the Blessed Virgin Mary."

Not knowing what to say, Brigid kept her mouth drawn in a tight line.

"I thought by now you'd be locked up in the nunnery." He assessed her from top to bottom. "Their loss could be my gain."

"Step aside, if you please," said Brigid, regaining her voice.

"Actually, I don't please," Stewart replied. "You're the prettiest thing I've seen in this town in a long time. I'm going to enjoy soaking up the view for a bit."

Brigid resisted looking over her shoulder towards the buggy. She'd have to figure out how to handle this herself — she had no desire to alarm Jeremiah.

Not that she wanted to engage in conversation with the oaf, but curiosity got the better of her and it gave her a moment to figure out how to elude him.

"Stewart, I've been back from school for several weeks and you're the only man of age I've seen not in uniform. Why aren't you serving our country like the other men?"

"That's a good question. You were at that hoity-toity finishing school, so you probably didn't hear of my mishap last fall." He paused for effect. "Of course, I enlisted like all those other men, but things just didn't work out as I had planned. Took a big spill when I was harness racing at the fairgrounds and got so banged up that I wasn't fit to serve. The men shipped out while I was still under the doctor's care." Stewart placed a hand on his back and winced. "I'm not sure my back will ever be quite the same."

Didn't work out as he planned, my foot, thought Brigid. *No one gets hurt harness racing. The horses never went faster than a trot.* She eyed him suspiciously. The man looked perfectly sound to her. She didn't bother voicing her doubts because she didn't want to give the cur any more of her time.

Stewart continued, "Besides, I've secured a new position, so I'm helping the cause just the same. Have you ever heard of a bounty hunter? A man can make a substantial living tracking down lost property. There're other endeavors tied to that position that are rather lucrative as well, but I won't hurt your sensibilities by going into any more detail. Let's just say we're paid to discourage folks from attempting to escape their masters and dissuade the do-gooders from aiding and abetting those felons."

Her eyes widened as the meaning of his words sunk in. Once again, she tried stepping around him, but he continued to block her path.

"I'm not a youngster anymore, Stewart. You can't pull your childish pranks on me."

"I'm not pulling a prank, just trying to get a little more of your time." He examined her once again, and his look was anything but moral. "Seeing you here, I was struck with a thought. You're done with school, all polished up and not in the nunnery, so I'd say that makes you fair game. Close as I can figure, I'm the best thing this town has going for it. A little thing like you could use a man like me to take care of her. These are some dangerous times we're living in."

"I beg your pardon," Brigid exclaimed.

She moved to her right and stepped off the edge of the boardwalk onto the street. "The only dangerous thing in this town is you."

"You may very well be right about that," said Stewart as he tipped his hat towards her and turned to go on his way.

Chapter X

Daylight seems to last forever when a person is trapped in a room until nighttime, mused Dominic. It was bad enough he wasn't allowed to leave the twelve-foot square area, but he couldn't make any noise. In addition to that, he had to stay out of view of the window so no one would spy him from outdoors, and thus he was forced to spend most of the day sitting on the hardwood floor in the corner of the room.

If more memories came back to him at least he'd have something to occupy his mind. On the other hand, if he had complete control of his faculties, he wouldn't be in this situation in the first place. He would return to where he belonged, wherever that was.

Dominic kept rehashing the few memories that had come to him to see if he could draw out any more tidbits of his life up to this point. He thought through them numerous times, yet nothing new came to light.

It was particularly irksome that he couldn't remember any more about Nathan whom, from what he gathered, was his closest acquaintance. Were they still friends? Was he fighting this battle as well? What became of him?

Maybe the man had a wife and children. For all Dominic knew, maybe *he* had a wife and children. There was no piece of gold circling his ring finger, but if he was a soldier perhaps he left the ring behind for safe keeping. That thought made him realize he needed to be cautious around Brigid. It was so easy falling for a girl like her. She was beautiful inside and out. Plus, that glimmer of spunk he saw in her made her even more attractive — she'd certainly keep a fellow on his toes.

Choosing not to dwell on her at that moment, Dominic looked around the room. He saw a shelf lined with books of various sizes. The only way he could get close enough to inspect the contents was by getting down on his hands and knees and crawling across the Oriental carpeting. That movement made his head pound, but he was getting antsy sitting in one spot for so long.

Reaching the shelf, he pulled a few books off and started thumbing through them. The first two were all printed words, so he put them back on the shelf. The next one appeared to be about horticulture — there were pictures of plants on almost every page. The topic wasn't that enticing for him, but Dominic couldn't decipher the printed words in any of the other books. It was perplexing because he could read the Bible he had on his person and he could speak two languages but, apparently, he was only literate in one. He double checked the shelf to see if by some chance there were any books in German, but nothing was visible so the picture book would have to do.

As the morning wore on, the room got warmer, which caused Dominic's head to nod as he perused the book. He couldn't get over how exhausted he was. *Must be the knock to the skull. Just wish it would've knocked some sense into me rather than knocking me senseless.*

After fighting off sleep as long as he could, his chin hit his chest and the book slid to the floor. Unlike the previous bouts of rest, there was no linear pattern to the dreams that came to him this time. Scenes from various periods of his life flashed through his mind.

He saw himself riding full out on a palomino, neck and neck with Nathan. A black and white checked border collie was trying to keep up with them. The sun felt warm on his face and the wind ran through his collar-length hair. He leaned forward in the stirrups and slapped the horse on its hindquarters in an effort to reach the line of hickory trees before Nathan. A feeling of euphoria washed over him as his ride edged out the other horse by a nose.

Horses were present in the next vignette as well. This time it was a team of four Belgians pulling an oversized cart. Bench seats ran from back to front on both sides of the vehicle. He and Nathan were packed into the space with a good twenty other men — ranging in age from teen to maybe mid-thirties. Catching snippets of conversation amongst the other occupants, he learned that they were heading to the old Red River Railway train depot.

The Red River rang a bell with him. Somehow he knew the Red River was a tributary of the Mississippi River and formed the eastern border between Texas and the Indian Territories. He recalled fetching water from that channel to bring to a dogtrot house. It was an ungodly hot day; the buzzing of cicadas rang in his ears, and he hurried to enter the breezeway between the two cabins to escape the heat.

The heat had been unbearable for months on end. Rounding up the Texas Longhorns, he and Nathan kept their mouths covered with bandanas to prevent breathing in any more dust than they had to. Throughout the day they removed their high-crowned, wide-brimmed hats and pulled the bright cloth handkerchiefs up to wipe their brows and stem the flow of sweat running into their eyes. That was nothing compared to the heat produced when they branded the new calves in the spring. He had the unenviable job of wrestling the young steers down so Nathan could apply the ND stamp to their flanks.

At some point, Dominic was ready to call "Uncle" and let the calf win for once, but there were no breaks working on a ranch. When you were your own boss, you couldn't take any shortcuts if you wanted your place to be profitable. Nathan, with the help of his brother-in-law

Jacob, put up the majority of cash for the purchase of Heavenly Vista Ranch. Dominic pitched in every red cent he had for his stake in the enterprise. He used the money he'd scraped together over the course of three years engaged in service as a hired hand in Illinois. Three hundred acres may not have seemed like a lot to some people, but it meant the world for the two young men. He was proud of what he and Nathan had accomplished — he doubted many other nineteen and twenty-year-olds had the wherewithal, determination and brute strength to even consider such an undertaking.

Uncertainty was a way of life for farmers and ranchers. So much depended on the weather, insects, disease — things that were out of their control. With a sense of hope, each spring they planted wheat, hay and a variety of vegetables to store up for the cold months.

Windstorms, drought, grasshoppers, critters — you never knew what could wipe out a whole season of work. It was the never-ending talk amongst the ranchers at the grange. That, and secession once the war started.

War? The country was at war, Dominic realized in his semi-conscious state. He dug deep into his memory banks to remember who was involved in the conflict. Had the English returned to establish the sovereignty of King Edward VII? Perhaps the French were intent on reclaiming the Louisiana Purchase, realizing the foolishness of selling nearly a million acres of land for just pennies per acre. The property he and Nathan had settled on was part of that historic transaction.

Neither of those scenarios made sense because they didn't involve secession, which was a voluntary act. The date November 6, 1860 came to his mind. It was branded there because it was the date the first Republican candidate was ever elected to the presidency of the United States —

Abraham Lincoln, ran on the platform in opposition to the expansion of slavery in the United States. While receiving only forty percent of the popular vote, the man handily beat his opponents due to the split between the Northern Democrats and the Southern Democrats.

One month later, seven states seceded from the Union — South Carolina, Mississippi, Florida, Alabama, Georgia, Louisiana, and Texas. Civil War was proclaimed on April 12, 1861, after Fort Sumter in Charleston, South Carolina, was bombarded by Confederate troops. Immediately thereafter, four slave states — Virginia, Arkansas, North Carolina and Tennessee — joined the burgeoning Confederate States of America.

Everything was flooding back to him now — leaving Illinois with Nathan to stake their claim in Texas, the back-breaking work of starting a ranch from scratch, driving cattle to the stockyards in Kansas City, clearing land for crops, building a homestead, supplying meat to the Confederate Army, hiding their loyalty to the Union.

The biggest revelation was recalling when he and Nathan received their conscription notice. By early 1864, the South was in short supply of everything it needed to conduct a war properly — including men. Under orders from Colonel Alfred Harris Abernathy, all able-bodied men ages thirty-five and under were to report for active duty.

Up to that point, he and Nathan had managed to defer themselves from service by providing dried, smoked or salted meat to the Confederate troops on active duty. However, diseases like dysentery and infirmities like diarrhea were killing twice as many soldiers as were being lost on the battlefields, so the Rebel commanders needed fresh meat of the human sort. Increasing the age of deployment and bringing in the stragglers who had somehow managed to elude the initial conscription notice would help build their stores once again.

Thus began their military career. He and Nathan left Heavenly Vista Ranch, their friends who worked for them, and the life they had grown to love behind them. The one thing neither of them left behind, he recalled, was a sweetheart.

Chapter XI

Meeting Stewart on the boardwalk rattled Brigid, but she wasn't going to let that deter her from her tasks. After taking a glance to assure herself that the man was walking in the opposite direction of her next destination, she stepped back onto the walkway and hurried down to the general store.

Normally she'd visit with Mr. Gilmore for a few minutes after she chose her items, but she had no time today, thanks to Stewart. She wanted to get to The Church of the Purification of the Blessed Virgin Mary as soon as morning Mass was finished. Brigid knew Father Barron would stay in the sacristy for at least a few minutes before heading off to work on his agenda for the day. Many times that meant leaving the property to care for parishioners in their time of need. It was imperative that she meet with him today. Brigid could only conceal the soldier for so long before someone stumbled across him.

Quickly she went through the candy sticks in the glass jar on the counter. She found the horehound piece and then grabbed the stick next to it for Martha. It was lemon, but it could have been any flavor, for all the little girl cared. Martha had a penchant for sweets of all design — Brigid had never seen her youngest sister turn down anything sugary.

She deposited a penny into Mr. Gilmore's hand, said a hasty goodbye, and walked out the door. A little bell on a piece of string chimed as the door slammed behind her. Checking the pocket watch in her reticule, she saw that it was almost time for Mass to end. As tempting as it would have been to pick up her skirts and run down the sidewalk, she resigned herself to walking at as quick of a pace as she could without drawing undue attention.

As she crossed the street, Jeremiah started to step down

from his perch on the buggy so he could help her onto the seat.

She waved him back. "No need for assistance, Jeremiah," she said. "I can get up by myself, thank you."

The man looked at her quizzically but did as he was told. Once she secured her spot, she instructed him to drive to the church posthaste.

Jeremiah cracked his whip above the horse's head, setting the animal off at a brisk pace. They went two blocks up Main Street then made a right turn toward the parish. Three blocks down, they reached their destination, and Brigid readied herself to disembark before they came to a full stop.

"I'll be out shortly," she said to Jeremiah before jumping to the ground.

As Brigid approached the door to the sacristy, she felt a sense of unease. She wasn't accustomed to speaking with Father Barron anywhere other than the confessional or the front yard of the church property. She prayed he would still be there, divesting himself of the vestments he wore for Mass and taking care of washing the Communion chalice and paten. If she didn't catch him here, the only other place he could be this close to the end of Mass would be the rectory next door. Brigid didn't know if she had the nerve to approach him at his private residence.

Thankfully, after three sharp taps on the door frame that led into the sacristy, the priest opened the portal.

Brigid exhaled, relieved. "Pardon me, Father Barron, if it's not a bother, I wish to have a word with you privately."

"Of course, Miss Brigid." Father Barron stepped back and welcomed her in with a wave of his hand. "Come in. Would you care for a cup of tea? I can have the housekeeper get some water heated up – no coffee anymore, sorry to say."

"Father, thank you so much for your hospitality, but I'll have to pass. I have precious little time to spare this morning. With the measles outbreak in town, I would imagine you're in the same position."

"That is true, dear. I was just having the cart brought up so I can go visit with the McDougal family. Three of their youngsters were stricken with them this past week."

"Sorry to hear that, Father. Please pass along my best wishes for a complete recovery."

"I will do that, Miss Brigid." He rolled his eyes upward to the left as though he were adding it to a list in his head. "Now, what brings you here this morning?"

"Father," said Brigid hesitantly, "I'm looking for counsel about a sensitive subject."

He looked at her with concern in his eyes. "Of course, Miss Brigid. I'm happy to help."

Not knowing where to begin, Brigid blurted out an abbreviated version of her story. "I found a man, a soldier actually, in our side yard early yesterday morning. My father is out of town, so I've hidden him in my father's study. Now I need advice about what to do with him."

The priest knit his brows together and leaned closer to her. "Would this, perhaps, be something better disclosed in the confessional?" he asked in a hushed voice, nodding his head towards the church proper.

Heat crept up Brigid's cheeks. "No, Father. My intentions are truly honorable, believe me."

"As you wish," he replied. "Could you perhaps enlighten me further as to why you felt compelled to hide this person?"

"That's a very good question with somewhat of a

Amanda Lauer

complicated answer," noted Brigid. She went on to describe what she knew of the man and how he had lost his memory from a blow to the head. The dilemma arose, she explained, because she wasn't sure where to send the soldier that would be safe and allow him time to recuperate from his disheveled mental state.

"You were right about it being a complicated situation, Miss Brigid," said Father Barron. "I know your heart is in the right place and you want to do what is best for the man. Let's talk through this and see if we can come up with a sensible solution."

He started ticking off considerations one finger at a time. "The only doctor we have in town is more accustomed to working with animals than humans, so I'm not sure what treatment he would prescribe for the man. You said you suspected the soldier may be a man listed as Missing in Action. There really is no practical way to track down the 53rd Tennessee or any other regiment, for that matter, because they are continually on the move. If we did know their location, it would be dangerous approaching the frontline." He tapped his next finger. "There is a lunatic asylum a couple of hours' ride from here, which could be a prudent place to send him."

Brigid looked at the priest with widened eyes. "Good Lord, I would say not. The poor man is injured, not insane." The thought of sending anyone to one of those institutions sent shivers down her spine.

Father rolled his eyes up to the left again as he pondered. "Allowing the man to recuperate at your residence would only be an option if it was short-term. We wouldn't want to take the chance of tarnishing your reputation. I would offer to let him stay with me until he's regained his senses but I've been exposed to so many people suffering from the measles lately, I wouldn't want to put him at risk for catching them."

The priest sat in silence for a minute as he tried to come up with other alternatives. He made the Sign of the Cross and bowed his head.

"O most holy apostle, Saint Jude, faithful servant and friend of Jesus, the Church honoreth and invoketh thee universally, as the patron of hopeless causes, and of things almost despaired of. Pray for me, who am so miserable."

He waited a moment to discern something. The man looked so intense Brigid swore he was receiving an audible answer. She couldn't hear anything. After a moment, Father Barron looked towards the heavens and said, "Thank you, Saint Jude." Apparently, the priest and the good saint were on a first-name basis.

Brigid stared at the priest and waited to hear his revelation.

"Has Saint Jude given you direction?" she whispered.

"Of course," answered Father Barron. "He always does."

"And that direction would be...?"

"I have business in Atlanta this week. I will have the soldier travel with me. It's a two-day trek. If the man is still without his memory when we arrive there, I'll bring him to the Confederate Hospital run by Dr. Burgess. You won't find a more skilled physician than him anywhere in the state," noted the priest.

"On the chance the man does regain his wits, then the destination will be the Church of the Immaculate Conception. Father O'Reilly will help him get back to the front. It's widely known that Father has clearance to walk into any camp, Union or Confederate. He attends to the spiritual needs of men on both sides of the conflict. If anyone can make sure the soldier is delivered safely back to a Confederate regiment, it would be him."

Saint Jude really did come through. I'll have to keep his

services in mind for future reference. The plan sounded so straightforward, how could there be any chance of failure? However, there was only one hitch, *or make that two.*

"Father, how will you deliver the man to Atlanta without anyone questioning why a priest would be traveling with a soldier? Someone may get the wrong idea and think you're assisting a deserter. Plus, you mentioned being around so many people with the measles. Would it be advisable for him to sit by your side for two days straight?"

"We have that covered," said Father, pointing up to the sky. "I've got the ideal mode of transportation for him that will keep him safe and that no one would dare question — a hearse. Trust me; we won't have to worry about anyone poking around inside of that."

The idea sounded nothing less than macabre to Brigid.

"Hearses have windows on all four sides. The man would still be visible."

"Not if he was inside a casket," said Father, shaking his pointer finger side to side.

"Please tell me there won't be another occupant sharing the ride," Brigid implored.

"Of course not, dear. There isn't that much elbow room."

She was relieved to hear that. Thinking about the plan, it seemed a bit risky to her, but they had precious few options and she wanted Dominic out of the house that evening.

"Thank you so much for your guidance, Father. I'll bring the soldier by after midnight tonight."

"Not so fast, young lady. You must have a little patience. My schedule does not permit me to leave any time before Wednesday."

"Wednesday, as in five days from today?" Brigid asked with a note of panic in her voice. "What am I to do with him until then?"

"Have faith, young lady. God will guide you."

Guide me, all right — straight to the stockade.

Chapter XII

It seemed an eternity before darkness finally fell and the door to the study cracked open again. Dominic wasn't sure how Brigid felt about him, but he was certainly happy to see her — and it wasn't just because of the provisions she brought. Who needed food when he could feast his eyes on her lovely face?

Brigid crouched down as she neared the sofa. The moonlight touched her hair and brought out the various hues of dark brown and deep mahogany. It looked so silky smooth that Dominic was tempted to reach out and touch it. He caught a whiff of rose water emanating from the locks, which looked as though they had been freshly washed that evening. The scent was mesmerizing.

I may be recovering my memories, but I'm as daft as a schoolboy when I'm around this Fraulein, he chided himself. With what he now remembered about his background, he knew it would be pure foolishness to set his sights on her. They both needed to get on with their lives. Even if Brigid had some interest in him, which seemed unlikely after their encounter the previous day, it was unacceptable and could even be dangerous for a Southern lady to be caught fraternizing with a Union soldier — which he planned on being once he figured out how to make the switch. He refused to put her in such a compromising position.

"How are you feeling this evening?" she inquired in a low tone.

"The headache has lessened," replied Dominic. He looked at her closely. She seemed suspiciously nice. Maybe she was hoping to depart on good terms when she had him escorted off the property later.

"Let me be more specific. Have any more memories come back to you?"

Dominic was loathe to be dishonest with Brigid. Lying was a venial sin, and he had no idea when he'd be able to get to confession again. He tried to remember which would require less penance, a sin of commission or a sin of omission. He hoped it was the latter.

"Bits and pieces," he said cryptically.

She looked at him, her eyes widening, as though she expected to hear more, so he continued. "I'm recalling tidbits from my childhood that aren't relevant to my current situation." He aimed to give her an answer that was vague yet provided enough information so that she wouldn't feel compelled to press him any further on the subject.

Apparently, that worked because she looked less than happy with his response.

After a moment of silence, Dominic decided to steer the conversation in another direction.

"And yourself? How are you feeling?"

"Oh, I'm just dandy."

The tone implied anything but to Dominic.

"Something I should know?" he asked.

"Well, let's see," said Brigid. "Would you like the good news first or the bad news?"

"I'll take the good news. After two days living in this box, I could use a little cheer. What have you got for me?"

"I met with Father Barron today at church. We talked through various options for you, and he came up with several ideas."

"I'm on pins and needles. Continue."

"We were thinking of transporting you to the nearest

lunatic asylum. It could be a satisfactory place for you to cool your heels while you wait for your memory to reestablish itself."

Dominic's eyebrows shot up, and his eyes opened wide in alarm. If that truly was the plan, then the ruse would be up — he'd turn himself in. No one came out of an insane asylum less crazy than when they entered the place. Those places were notorious for their maltreatment of patients — under the guise of advancing the science of illnesses of the mind. *I'll skedaddle to the nearest Rebel camp and beg them to send me back to the front before I'll consent to that idea.*

Squinting, he looked closer at the girl. *Was that a smile forming on her lips? Was she making a joke at my expense?*

Brigid covered her mouth with her hand as though concealing a yawn, but she couldn't hide the merriment in her eyes upon seeing his reaction.

"Well, aren't we the humorous one?" Dominic said with a hint of irritation in his voice.

"We try," replied Brigid.

"I'm sure we do, Your Majesty."

He motioned his hand to get her to continue.

Brigid picked up where she left off. "Seeing that I, um... Father Barron wasn't comfortable with such a plan, we came up with something that should be feasible and keep you out of harm's way until your bearings are intact once again."

Clearing her throat lightly, Brigid went on. "Father Barron has kindly offered to transport you to Atlanta. You can receive top-notch medical care at a hospital in the city or if, by chance, your memory does come back to you, then Father will escort you to Immaculate Conception Church. Father O'Reilly is the pastor there and he's been a neutral party in this conflict, so he'll be able to get you back to a Confederate camp in no time."

Dominic considered that option. Other than the last part about going back to the side of the Rebels, which he had no intention of doing, it seemed solid enough to him. If the priest was able to get him into a Confederate camp, he certainly should be able to get him into a Union camp as well.

"However, with your well-being in mind, you can't be seen riding next to Father Barron on the wagon — it would certainly raise questions as to why a soldier, who appeared to be of good health, would be wandering the countryside with a parish priest. Father has devised a clever plan to conceal you from any people or patrols you may encounter. You'll be traveling in the parish hearse down to Atlanta — or more specifically in a coffin inside the hearse. No one would consider checking the contents of a casket, especially with the measles outbreak right now.

The thought of being confined inside that tight of a space made his skin crawl. Considering the cadaver who may be the next tenant of the casket caused a trickle of sweat to run along his temple all the way to his jaw line. He swore he heard the salty water make a tiny splash as it hit his left hand.

Working to regain his composure, he said, "Now I can see why you said there was good news and bad news.

"Oh, that's not the bad news," said Brigid in a somber tone. "We have a bigger problem than that."

"There you go with the Royal We again," complained Dominic, "unless you plan on occupying those confines with me."

She chose to ignore his grievance. "The bad news," she said in a grave voice, "is that Father Barron cannot leave town until Wednesday. That means you'll be in my care for four more days."

Her serious tone almost made Dominic laugh. He did his best to maintain a neutral countenance, but he was almost giddy over his fortune. Chances were they would never encounter each other again, so he was overjoyed at the thought of getting to spend an extended amount of time with her.

As a Unionist, he would have no chance of courting her as long as the war dragged on. Her father would probably rather see him dead than involved with his progeny. But he wanted to depart in her good graces — before she had a chance to find out his true identity.

If Brigid did end up joining the convent, as a bride of Christ she could put a good word in for him, maybe call on the saints to watch over him. He would take whatever protection he could get to make it through his military career alive.

In the meantime, that gave him four extra days to see what kind of plan he could come up with on his own to either convince Father O'Reilly to deliver him to the Union side or to make his escape once they were in Atlanta. There was no way on God's green earth he was going to be offering his services to the Confederate Army. They forced him to do it once; it wasn't going to happen again. He and Nathan had vowed to get themselves to a Union Army camp as soon as they found the opportunity to do so. Knowing how clever his friend was, Dominic was fairly certain Nathan had already accomplished that goal. Now he needed to do the same. From there the plan was to stay alive, finish out the war, and then make it back to the ranch.

Both men had dreamed of reuniting with the friends they'd left behind who were working the property in their absence — the free black Ol' Joe, Eduardo and his wife Maria who ran the house, and their Cherokee compadre, Snapping Turtle. If fate failed them and only one made it back alive, the entire operation would go to the survivor. If neither of them made it through the war, the estate would be split evenly between the three men overseeing the property. They had the brains and competence to keep the operation running.

Brigid backed away from the sofa. As she did, her hand brushed into the book Dominic had been looking through during the day. Picking it up, she peered at it closely and read the title out loud. "*Flower-Garden; Breck's Book of Flowers; in Which are Described all the Various Hardy Herbaceous Perennials, Annuals, Shrubby Plants, and Evergreen Trees, Desirable for Ornamental Purposes, With Directions for their Cultivation* by Joseph Breck, Seedsman and Florist, and Former Editor of the *New England Farmer* and *The Horticultural Register*.

"Good Lord, is this how you've been biding your time during the day? No wonder you're batty," said Brigid, with a shake of her head. "I've a selection of much more interesting tales on my bookshelf. There's *Pride and Prejudice, Jane Eyre, Wuthering Heights...*"

Not recognizing the titles, he made no reply. Brigid continued, "Of course, those may be too feminine for you. I also have a copy of *Frankenstein*. That should be to your liking. Or if you prefer something more contemporary, I received Alexandre Dumas' novel, *The Count of Monte Cristo*, on my last birthday. It's a follow-up to his book *The Three Musketeers*, which you may have already read."

Dominic wasn't sure how to respond to her suggestion. When he was a child, his *Mutter* taught him to read and write and decipher. Frau Warner demanded perfection from him, as she had been a well-respected schoolmarm when she was a young woman living in Deutschland before she married his *Vater*.

His handwriting was meticulous and his diction flawless

as he read his history and literature assignments to her. She always told him he was the most promising student she had ever worked with and assured him she wasn't showing favoritism. The woman had dreams of Dominic attending university in their new country and someday becoming a wealthy man.

Apparently, the education she aspired for him wasn't meant to be because he never stepped foot into a classroom after his parents passed. He was fluent in English, but he could not read or write in that language.

I'm already in enough hot water with the man upstairs; I can't afford to tell any more mistruths. After a moment of hesitation, he decided to share his secret with her, hoping she wouldn't mock him for being a dunce.

"Miss Brigid, it's kind of you to offer to share your books with me, it really is. But I need to confess something to you. He paused before blurting out, "I can only read and write in my native language."

"Oh," said Brigid. "Pardon me for making the assumption that you were literate in my language. You've had formal schooling, have you not?"

"Yes, miss," replied Dominic. "I was tutored by the best — my late *Mutter*."

"I'm sure she was an outstanding instructor." After pondering a moment, Brigid went on. "You obviously speak English well; it should be easy enough to transfer that knowledge to the written text. The one thing we have plenty of over the next few days is time. If you are open to this proposal, I would be willing to spend the next four evenings teaching you to read English. Assuming you're not an idiot, we should be able to get the basics into you before you leave."

Assuming I'm not an idiot. Apparently, she had never

met a drill sergeant — they lived under the supposition that all their underlings were imbeciles. He could still remember when he and his fellow recruits were berated by those sadistic officers when they first joined up with the 53rd. That was a memory he wouldn't share with Brigid — he didn't want her to think less of him, and, more importantly, he didn't want her to know he regained his memory.

Getting his train of thought on track again, he heard Brigid add, "Unless, of course, you're not up to the challenge."

Was she daring him to see if he could learn to read a new language in four days? Dominic wasn't sure if such a feat was possible or not, but he knew one thing — when he was offered a challenge, he never backed down.

Chapter XIII

There was no time like the present, so Brigid pulled a wall sconce down and lit it with a match from a holder on the fireplace mantel. Hoisting the light in front of her, she used it to guide her to her father's bookshelves. She knelt down and started looking closely at the titles. Many of the books were on the topics of history, farming and politics, but there were some random volumes, such as the one about the business of slave trading. None of them caught her interest.

She preferred to read romance novels. Her father always told her there was no need to fill her mind with men's business — if she needed to form an opinion on any topic of substance, he would do so for her. That was fine with her anyhow. The war was the most talked-about affair in the last four years, and she had lost interest in that a long time ago. She was just waiting for the hostilities to end so she could get on with her life. If things could be resolved before autumn, even better — then more options would be available for her to continue her education.

It wasn't that she objected to entering the religious life, but the decision felt rushed, which did not set well with her. But once her father got something in his head, nothing deterred him from carrying out his plans. So if he said she was going to join a religious order, then she would be joining a religious order come hell or high water. One could say she had a choice of which particular order to enter, but she had no idea what differentiated one group from the next.

Getting back to her task, she walked her fingers along the edges of the books one by one, looking for something that may be of mutual interest to her and Dominic. She got all the way to the bottom shelf before she finally hit her mark — *Great Expectations* by Charles Dickens. It was a book she had wanted to read for some time. She didn't realize her father owned a copy. Actually, she couldn't recall seeing him ever reading for pleasure, so she was somewhat surprised to find the tome amongst the stodgy books that lined the rest of the shelves. But that was neither here nor there, the story would be ideal for her to read with Dominic because the subject was one said to be of interest to both males and females.

Pulling it off the shelf, she went back to Dominic, who was sitting on the floor in front of the sofa. Apparently, he didn't want to take a chance and be spotted — not that any soul would be wandering the grounds this time of the night. He patted the floor next to him as an invitation for her to sit down. She put the sconce near his leg and settled herself down a good foot on the other side of it. Brigid wasn't comfortable positioning herself too close to him — she recalled the feeling she experienced when he brushed into her arm the other night. Thinking about that still made her blush.

Opening the book, she decided to point out the easy, one-syllable words that needed to be memorized, like "a," "the" and "she" to start the lesson. Dominic picked those up quickly enough. Then she had him repeat and sound out two-syllable words. Once he was to that point, she decided to start reading the book to him as quietly as possible and run her finger under each word so he could start reading along. Every so often when she saw a word that she figured he could pronounce she would have him read it out loud to her. As unexpected as it seemed, it actually felt quite comfortable being near him, and she couldn't help but laugh when he added his droll commentary to the story.

Two hours in, she was starting to feel the effects of the

long day, so she found a scrap of paper from her father's desk to use as a bookmark and inserted it in the book. Turning to Dominic, she promised to pick up where they left off when she came back the next night.

After leaving Dominic, Brigid went to bed and fell asleep with a smile on her face, dreaming of the fine-looking soldier camped out in her father's study. She was able to get a few hours of sleep in before she was awakened by the sound of her little sisters racing through the house playing a game of tag. Back in the day, her mother would have nipped such unladylike behavior in the bud, but she didn't seem to have the energy anymore to do anything other than sit in a winged-back chair in the parlor and work on her stitching. The girls could be stomping up and down the curved foyer stairway like elephants or chasing each other out of the house, with the woven wire door slamming in their wake, yet, other than an occasional glance, Mrs. McGinnis kept her eyes fixed on the embroidery threads before her.

Looking to kill two birds with one stone, Brigid decided to take the girls on a walk and have a picnic lunch with them. That would help them burn off some energy and make the time pass by more quickly. It seemed to take forever for the light to be totally extinguished from the sky each evening this time of year, so she had many hours to fill before the occupants of the house were all abed and she could meet with Dominic again.

Brigid couldn't stop thinking about the man. She tried to convince herself that she was just concerned about his welfare but in her heart, she knew that wasn't true. It was discomfiting to admit, but she was attracted to him. It wasn't just the fact that he cut such a handsome figure, it was so many things about him — he was smart, he was funny, he was gentle. The list could go on and on if she put her mind to it, but she realized there was no point in daydreaming like a schoolgirl. For some reason, known only to God, the two of their lives crossed paths. But it was just a chance encounter and soon she would need to resume the journey her father laid out for her. Dominic would need to get back to his life as well — whatever that turned out to be.

Grabbing the picnic basket the cook had filled for them, Brigid strolled out the back door with Agnes and Martha following behind her like two little ducklings. She intended to walk beyond their barn to the closest neighbor's farm. When they were at church on Sunday, Mr. Martin told them that his ewe had a late-season birth and produced triplets. He invited them over to see the baby lambs.

The girls wanted to go that very day, but Brigid thought it would be better to wait until the lambs were at least ten days old before they walked over. If they survived that long, chances were they'd make it to adulthood — but there wasn't anything much cuter than tiny baby lambs so she didn't want to delay too long.

A grove of trees stood between the properties. They had a path they took between the two places, and she and her sisters set off in that direction. When they reached the beech trees, Brigid noticed a notch cut into the big tree on the edge of their property. It looked to be manmade, which was puzzling.

Walking into the copse further, she found another notch in a tree and, like the first one, it was waist-high on her. It almost looked like someone was marking a path through the woods. Brigid couldn't imagine who would be walking between the two properties other than the families who lived there. Yet none of them would have a reason to mark a path they had walked more times than they could count.

Trees were notched about every twenty feet and led through the entire grove and stopped at the wooden post and nail fence that marked the border of Mr. Martin's land. Brigid didn't mention anything to her sisters. They were preoccupied with getting to the fence and scooting under it so they could approach the lambs nuzzling their mama's underside, looking for milk.

After the girls had their share of time with the little creatures, they went back outside the fenced-in area. Brigid laid out a quilt for them to sit on and poured water from the copper pitcher onto each of their hands to make sure their fingers were clean before they started eating lunch.

After they ate and packed up again, they headed back towards their house. Walking through the trees, Brigid realized the markings were only visible from one direction. It was so odd that they were there in the first place. No one in her family would have done something like that, and she couldn't imagine why any of the servants would have a need to do such a thing either.

Maybe it was just a coincidence and the markings were from a woodpecker trying to get under the bark of the tree. In the whole scheme of things, it didn't really matter anyhow and it wasn't worth putting any more energy into thinking about it. The fresh air, sunshine and lack of sleep for the past few nights made her long for a good nap. After she got back from confession that afternoon, she would curl up with Martha on the four-poster bed and get some rest for an hour or two. She wanted to be at her best when she resumed the reading lesson with Dominic.

The nap and the delicious fried chicken dinner Beulah prepared for supper did a world of good for Brigid. She was able to discreetly wrap a chicken leg in a napkin to surprise Dominic later. More than likely, he was getting tired of bread and water by this point.

When she finally was able to get to the study later that night, Dominic ate the scrawny appendage with gusto. There wasn't anything left but the bone by the time he was done. Brigid felt somewhat guilty because he looked so hungry when she had handed it to him. She'd have to see if she could find him something more substantial the next time she foraged through the pantry. Maybe there was some leftover jarred fruit from last fall in the root cellar. The place gave her the creeps, but if she went down there during the day when it was sunny it would be less ominous — as long as she was in and out quickly.

After Dominic licked every finger clean, he wiped his hands on the napkin and folded it neatly into a square. Reaching toward the sofa, he grabbed the book they were reading and surprised her by announcing that he had been working on the story throughout the day.

Opening the book, he haltingly began to read, sounding out the words as he went. "I loved her against reason, against promise, against peace, against happiness, against all..." He hesitated and looked toward her. Brigid's cheeks were aflame. She quickly turned away and glanced at the book.

"Discouragement," she supplied, enunciating each syllable.

"Against all discouragement that could be," he concluded.

Brigid wasn't sure how to react to the paragraph he read. Was he teasing her by reading something so amorous or by coincidence was that the spot at which he left off earlier in the day? She gave him a sideways glance. He looked so pleased with himself that she assumed it was the latter. She complimented him on his fine reading skills.

"I'm impressed at how quickly you're picking this up," she said.

"It's actually not as difficult as I had imagined it would be once I set my mind to it," Dominic said. "Besides, the letters in English are the same as German, so it's not like I'm trying to decipher hieroglyphics."

"Very true." Still feeling a bit out of sorts after hearing that passage, Brigid suggested perhaps it would be best if she left him for the evening so he could continue practicing on his own.

Dominic had another suggestion. "How about we take a break from reading and talk for a bit? Would that be agreeable to you?"

It would be more than agreeable, thought Brigid, *anything to extend our time together*. She didn't want to seem forward, so she hesitated before politely accepting his invitation.

"Have you had a breakthrough?" she asked with hope in her voice. "Is that why you want to talk? Have more pieces of your memory been put back into place?"

"Not really," said Dominic. "He hesitated before continuing. "What I wanted to say is... we've been acquainted for a couple of days now, and I'd like to get to know you better. Could you tell me more about your family? Maybe start with your father. It sounds like he is quite an influence in your life."

"That is correct," she said, wondering where the course of his questioning would lead but answering him nonetheless. "He's not around much nowadays with the war. He spends most of his time in Richmond in his role as the Secretary of the Interior for President Davis."

"Secretary of the Interior. That sounds impressive. How did he land that role?" Dominic asked.

"That's a fair question. He was asked by President Davis to be a member of his cabinet. If he had his druthers, my father would have taken on the role of Secretary of State, but Mr. C.G. Memminger had accepted that position shortly after the war started. Actually, by the time my father made the decision to accept any post, all the cabinet spots were filled. Seeing that President Abraham Lincoln had a Secretary of Interior and Treasury, and with a desire to have the financial backing of my father, President Davis created a similar position in his cabinet for him," said Brigid.

"What are the duties of the Secretary of the Interior?" asked Dominic.

"I really couldn't tell you," said Brigid. "I'm not so sure my father even knew what they would be when he accepted the position, but it does sound quite important, doesn't it? He appreciates prestigious titles."

Hearing that, Dominic chuckled.

"I have a mother, as well, and I'm the eldest child. My parents had two girls and a boy after me."

"You're lucky. I was an only child. With my parents gone, I have no family here that I'm aware of."

"Again, I'm sorry to hear that you lost your parents. You said they died when you were fourteen, what year was that?"

"1853," said Dominic without pause.

"Oh, then you have regained some more memory if you can recall that. You're making progress, that's encouraging."

Dominic nodded.

She did the math in her head. If his birthday was in the first half of the year, that would make him twenty-five years old, just seven years older than Brigid. That age suited him, *and her*, she admitted to herself.

"That was the year of the cholera epidemic. Did they succumb to that?"

"No. It was a house fire."

"Oh my, I'm so sorry to hear that. Thank goodness you survived."

Dominic sat in silence for a moment. "If it wasn't for me, they'd still be alive," he said in a somber voice.

"What? You can't be serious, can you?"

After a moment, he answered. "I've never told this story to anyone, not even in the confessional, but *meine Mutter und Vater* died trying to save my life."

Brigid braced herself to hear his story.

Dominic let out a sigh and began. "My father was a sharecropper and worked on various farms throughout his adult life. My mother and I followed him and the work. One day my father was plowing a field and my mother and I were with him, performing my least-favorite chore — picking rocks from the rows as he went along. I left them with the excuse that I needed to get a ladle of water from the well to quench my thirst. It was actually an excuse to buy time from laboring in the field. So I meandered off. When I finally did get in sight of the house, I saw flames on the roof. Smoke was starting to billow from the structure." He hesitated a few seconds and then continued.

"We had a cat that made its bed in the loft area where I slept. I knew she was trapped in there, so I ran to the house and climbed up the ladder to reach her. Before I could make my way to the back of the loft, I felt my mother take hold of my shirt and pull me to the edge of the loft where my father was there to grab me. He sent me out of the house. Over my shoulder, I saw him helping my mother down the ladder. The next thing I knew, the roof collapsed. They were unable to escape."

Brigid let the story sink in for a moment before she said anything.

"You certainly didn't mean for that to happen," she said quietly. "You mustn't blame yourself. It was an accident."

"The fire may have been an accident, but what I did was

pure stupidity. Once I got to the loft, the cat jumped down on its own and made its way out the open door. Cats have nine lives but, unfortunately, human beings have only one."

"Dominic," she said, "you can't continue to blame yourself. You were trying to save a life, not take one." Brigid had an urge to reach out and caress his cheek to brush the morose look off his face, but she dared not. It was too intimate of a gesture.

"What happened to you was a misfortune. Danger abounds on the frontier — who knows how that fire started. I would put money on it that if the tables had been turned and you saw your mother and father in peril, you would have done the same thing they did. They gave their lives for you. Now they can spend eternity as saints, as God's elect. You are fortunate to have two people who cared about you so much on this earth now interceding on your behalf in heaven."

There was a softening to Dominic's face. "I never thought of it that way," he admitted.

Brigid prayed he would take those words to heart. Now came the difficult part, voicing her darkest secret to a man she barely knew. This wouldn't be easy because she wasn't one to share personal secrets with anyone, but since he opened up first, she felt it would only be right to reciprocate.

"I have my own story to relay to you, but I have to warn you, this wasn't an accident. I wish to God it were, but I have no one to blame but myself." Grief brought a frown to her face as memories of *That Day* swarmed to the forefront of her mind.

"My brother John Thaddeus McGinnis II was born the summer before I started my ninth year of school. As the firstborn son, John was my father's pride and joy. We all loved him just as much. It was not easy for me to leave him when I had to return to the Lucy Cobb Institute that autumn. I couldn't wait to see him when I came home for Christmas break."

She took a deep breath and the picture of that dear infant came to her mind. "The day after I got home, my parents were hosting a Christmas gathering for their friends. After my sisters were escorted to bed, my mother sent John upstairs with the wet nurse. I asked my mother if I could rock the baby to sleep after he was fed. John was so sweet, I wanted to spend more time with him. My mother agreed, and so after the nurse left I sat in the rocker cradling him and singing him to sleep. Once he was soundly sleeping, I laid him on his stomach on my parent's bed. I positioned myself next to him and watched him as he slept. Before I knew it, I was asleep myself."

She hesitated as the next image was painful to think about. "After sleeping an hour or so, I woke up and the room seemed so still. I put my hand on John's back and his little body felt stiff. In the candlelight, I saw that his skin was ashen. I picked him up and tried shaking him to awaken him, but his eyes didn't open. I then ran with him downstairs. My father took one look at John and grabbed him from me. He then shouted, 'What have you done to him!?'"

A tear slowly slid down her cheek. "They fetched the doctor and when the man arrived, he said the baby died from suffocation. I swear I didn't roll over on him, but he died while in my charge, so it was my fault."

Telling the story brought back all the feelings Brigid had buried for so long — the fear, the guilt and the shame.

"I should go now. I can't imagine you want to spend any more time with me. I know my father certainly doesn't want to, that's why he's hell bent on having me join a religious order. He's right though. The convent would be the best place for me anyhow. I don't want to get married because marriage leads to children. One child has already died on my account. I couldn't bear to be faced with that situation again. I'd lose my mind, just like my mother did after John died."

Dominic looked at her with tenderness in his eyes. He reached out and engulfed her in his arms. Brigid couldn't help it; instinctively she put her head to his chest. The sound of his heart comforted her.

"*Schatzie*," he said as he pulled her tighter. "You told me that I wasn't at fault for what happened to my parents, so now I want you to hear me out. Not every baby survives infanthood. It's regrettable that your brother passed away at such a young age, but you yourself said you did nothing to cause his death. God chose to pluck John from this earth and it happened to be a moment while he was in your charge. Only He knows why."

Brigid took several deep breaths and tried to keep her shoulders from shaking. Dominic ran his hand through her hair in a calming fashion.

"Hearing your story makes my own seem more clear. You were not at fault; I was not at fault. I don't know why those things happened, but I do know that God had a plan for our loved ones and He has a plan for you and for me."

The tears Brigid had been holding back for more than two years flowed unchecked down her cheeks, soaking Dominic's cotton shirt. His words and the gentle caressing of her locks consoled her but also caused her to wonder. Dominic said that God had a plan for her and a plan for him, *but does He have a plan for us?*

Chapter XIV

Dominic held Brigid in his arms until the tears finally subsided and sleep overtook her. He never wanted to let go of her. If he could protect *siene Schatzie* for the rest of his life, he gladly would. But it didn't appear fate intended for them to be together much longer. When he saw the veil of darkness lifting from the earth, he knew he had to wake her and send her back upstairs before the members of the household got up for the day.

He kissed the top of her head and lightly ran his fingers over her cheek. Her skin was smooth as a flower petal and she had the faint aroma of roses about her, as she did the other night. When he started pulling away, the movement woke her and her eyes fluttered open. She touched her cheek as if remembering some sensation. Becoming more aware, Brigid stiffened and looked straight into Dominic's eyes. As she pushed herself away from him, their eyes remained locked. When she had adequate room, she rose and turned away, giving the excuse that she needed to line up the tasks for the household help for the day. She hastily departed his company.

According to her father's clock on the fireplace mantelpiece, Brigid did not come back to the room until well after midnight that night. She was strictly business when she came in — bringing more bread, water and fruit and giving Dominic the opportunity to stretch his legs and make his way to the convenience while she kept an eye out. There was no conversation between them. The next night and the night after that, the same routine was followed.

Who could say what was going through her mind, Dominic mused. Perhaps she regretted sharing such a personal story with him, or maybe she was ashamed for being so vulnerable in front of him. But rather than diminish his concern for her, that incident actually endeared her to him more. He wished things didn't have to end like this.

In the wee hours of the morning, Brigid came into the study dressed in what looked to be a black mourning gown. Dominic wondered if it was the dress she had worn for her brother's service. Over that was a black-hooded cape. She held a loaf of bread and the pitcher of water and handed them to Dominic without a word. As he sat down and started tearing into the loaf, an awkward silence hung between them. Dominic endeavored to imagine what she was thinking. Try as he might, he couldn't reign in the feelings he had for her. *Was she perhaps experiencing the same dilemma? Was that why she hadn't spoken to him for the last three nights?*

He continued to eat in silence. Knowing this was the day he was to meet with Father Barron, Dominic was aware that Brigid would have to speak up at some point so that he would know what their course of action would be.

"We'll leave as soon as you are finished," she said finally, breaking the silence.

Dominic nodded — he didn't want to talk with his mouth full and appear to be ill-mannered. She sounded as though she would rather leave sooner than later, so he resisted the temptation to break the bread into minuscule pieces to slow down the process and have more time in her company. Even if she was in no mood to talk, he wanted to remember every nuance of her face and body language. Someday when things got rough and he needed a sliver of hope to hang onto, he could return to her in his mind and reminisce about what could have been between them under different circumstances.

He had nothing to pack so when he was done eating, he

stood, dusted the crumbs off his lap and turned to Brigid.

"Follow me out of the house and we will walk to the rectory of The Church of the Purification of the Blessed Virgin Mary. Father Barron will be expecting us. It shouldn't take more than twenty minutes to get there." Brigid pulled the door open.

They walked through the hallway and kitchen with their path illuminated by one small candle burning on the side table. The pair exited the house through the back door. Once outside, Brigid paused, giving both of them time to let their eyes adjust to the darkness. She scanned the yard. Apparently satisfied with what she saw, she descended the two stairs to ground level and motioned for him to do the same. Keeping close to the side of the house, they followed the perimeter of the building to reach the front yard. When they made it out to the street, she quietly told him the route they would use that should lessen the chances of being stumbled upon by any townsperson.

As Dominic followed Brigid, the only sound he heard was their feet padding through the grass and the tree frogs offering their nighttime chorus for the audience of two. No words passed between them.

Fortune was on their side — they arrived at the rectory without encountering anyone. Brigid climbed the four steps to the entryway and lightly rapped on the wood panel. Within seconds, Father Barron opened the door and light flooded over them. Seeing who graced his doorstep, he swung it open wider and ushered the man and woman into his residence.

Hastily, Brigid made introductions between the two men. Dominic and Father Barron shook hands. Then the priest laid out his plan for their trip to Atlanta. Since it would take two days to get there by wagon, they would stop overnight at a parish where the rector was a trusted friend of his.

Noting the horse hitched up to the hearse already, Father Barron suggested they take their leave. Brigid gave her heartfelt thanks to the priest for taking care of Dominic. She held her hand out as though to offer the priest a handshake but when he extended his hand towards her, she turned it up and placed several gold dollar coins into his palm and then gently folded his fingers over them.

"Miss Brigid, I cannot accept money from you," exclaimed the priest. "I'm doing the work of God."

"I understand that, Father, but I want to express my gratitude to you for going out of your way to help us. However, if you feel you cannot use the money for yourself, then please use it to help some less fortunate soul."

"Thank you, miss. I will be sure to do that, and I will make sure they know who their benefactor is."

With the transaction complete, Brigid turned to Dominic, who was looking towards the priest.

"Father Barron, would you mind if I stepped outside with Miss Brigid for a moment?" he asked.

"That would be fine, son. I'll fetch the vehicle and bring it to the front."

He left them and headed towards the rear of the residence. When he was gone, Dominic held the door open and with a sweeping gesture, invited Brigid to walk out ahead of him. After they descended the stairs to ground level, he squared her towards him by putting one hand on each of her shoulders.

He looked down at her, drinking in what would probably be the last sight he would ever have of her.

"Brigid," he said, dropping formalities, "I don't know how I can ever thank you enough for what you've done for me."

She looked at him intently, slightly biting her lower lip,

which was beginning to tremble.

Dominic hated goodbyes — more times than not what was supposed to be a "so long for now" turned out to be a "so long forever." His heart ached as he saw Brigid's eyes misting over.

"I wish I could promise you that I would come back and find you someday. I don't want to cloud your judgment by making a pledge that I may not be able to fulfill. If you truly have a calling to the religious life, I need to respect that, regardless of my feelings towards you."

Her eyes widened.

"*Auf Wiedersehen, Schatzie*. I will never forget you."

She nodded, blinking back tears. When she finally found her voice she said, "Goodbye, Dominic. I'll treasure the memories of our time together. Do your best to stay safe."

"That, I promise you, I will. Of course, my guardian angel may have to step it up a bit — he's already slipped up once," he replied, giving her a wink.

"Perhaps it wasn't an oversight on their part. They say God works in mysterious ways — mayhap he excused him for a day so things could play out as they did. But either way, I'll pray that he stays at his task this time around," she replied, giving him a smile.

Dominic moved his hands up from her shoulders and gently placed one on each side of her face. He took a final look at her and leaning forward brushed his lips against hers in a tender kiss. "*Ich liebe dich*. You'll be in my prayers."

Chapter XV

Long after the hearse pulled away from the rectory, Brigid stood rooted to the ground, using the railing behind her as support. She replayed those last moments with Dominic over and over again in her head.

He genuinely seemed to care about her, which took her by surprise. She was by no means an expert on the topic, but it didn't seem like the kind of care a brother would show for a sister. It was more like the affection a young man would show his sweetheart.

Why me? There were so many comely girls to choose from. As the pool of eligible men dwindled, a man like him could have any girl he wanted.

Brigid considered herself from head to toe and found nothing spectacular of note. She had brown hair, darker than most, but nothing impressive from her point of view. Her eye color was somewhat unusual. Like her mother, she had green eyes, but Brigid's were significantly brighter and clearer. That being said, she doubted that Dominic, if pressed, would even know what color they were — most of their time together had been spent in near darkness.

Thinking of her figure, there were no two ways about it. She was petite — everywhere. It seemed to her that most men were attracted to women with voluptuous figures, the kind accentuated by the hoops and bustles currently in fashion. Being slender did have its advantages, though. Her waist was so trim that she could get by without the restricting corsets to which most women were subjected. The disadvantage was that she looked young — and there was nothing worse than being treated like a child when she was just months away from adulthood.

Next on the list was Brigid's complexion. Her skin was quite fair, unblemished and she had just a scant number of freckles on her pert nose, thanks to her vigilance in keeping her head covered on sunny days. Her teeth, which were similar in color to the pearls on her mother's favorite necklace, were somewhat small but they were straight and she had all of them. That was a plus.

Brigid had a deathly fear of the barbers who were paid to not only cut hair but pull teeth as well. She heard horror stories about them so, consequently, she was fastidious about caring for her teeth — she never wanted to be subjected to their ministrations. Every morning after breakfast and every evening before she turned in for the night she would clean her teeth using a cloth sprinkled with tooth powder. The gritty substance scrubbed each tooth clean, and the peppermint ground into the powder gave her breath a pleasant scent.

What did it matter what kind of teeth she had anyhow? she chided herself. Dominic wasn't looking for a horse. If he was like most honorable men, he was looking for a wife. No matter what fantasies she concocted, that woman would not be her. Dominic was gone and he wasn't coming back. It was time to admit that and get on with her life.

She was finally able to step away from the building and start her trek back to the house. Tracing the same path she and Dominic had walked just an hour earlier, she couldn't turn off the inner workings of her mind. What had he said to her in German immediately before he took his leave? She had never heard those words before, and she didn't know anyone who could translate them. Even if she did, she would sound foolish asking. It could have been something innocuous or something of substance. Chances were she'd never know.

She also wondered what the word *Schatzie* meant.

Several times throughout the week he had called her that. Was it a term of endearment? It sounded similar to the word sister, so was he teasing her when he called her that? Maybe the feelings he had toward her *were* brotherly in nature.

At this point, what difference did it make anyhow? The task she faced now was getting back to the house, catching some sleep, and discovering ways to bide her time until her father returned with her marching orders.

Brigid did manage to get a few hours of slumber that night, but it was restless. She could not shake the image of the brown-haired man with the striking eyes. Upon waking, she felt as though she barely slept a wink. The whole day dragged on. Brigid went through her duties of running the household and directing the staff by rote and politely covered her mouth each time she yawned. She wished her mother would snap out of her bad humor and resume her role as head of the household, so their lives could have some semblance of normality again.

If Father Barron had been in town, Brigid would have gone to church for confession. She had some things to get off her chest, but it was probably just as well because she didn't have the energy to make the trip into town anyway. She was physically and mentally drained.

Since confession was out of the picture, she decided to spend time with her sisters — she snuggled up for an afternoon nap with the two of them for a couple of hours. Certainly God would be pleased to see her giving them some much-needed attention.

In her room later that night, she didn't even bother to put on her nightdress. The nap had given her a second wind, and on top of that, she was feeling restless. As she sat in the Empire chair, she mulled over all that had transpired since she first encountered Dominic.

She recalled their conversation about baby John. As hard as it had been to acknowledge that transgression, she was reassured by his reaction. His words did give her grounds to think she had been blaming herself for the child's death without just cause.

When she had confessed her mortal sin to Father Barron shortly after the incident, he said she was forgiven in the name of God the Almighty Father and then doled out a hefty penance. But he never said she was without blame. No one except Dominic had ever indicated that to her.

Maybe he *should go into the religious life*, she thought wryly. Thinking back to the kiss he had bestowed on her, a warm sensation enveloped her that made her reconsider that notion. A virile man like him deserved a woman who could match his strength and passion for life. But doubts overshadowed that thought. Even if the stars completely aligned in her favor, she wasn't sure if she was up to that undertaking.

Considering marriage made her think of children. She missed little John so much; regardless of what happened, she still had a fondness for babies. But unless something in her life changed dramatically over the next half year, she would never be a mother. Brigid wasn't sure how she felt about that now.

Thinking back to her little brother, she remembered his smiles and the way he babbled. He was so adorable when he'd pull his legs up to his chest and suck on his little baby toes. Even when he wasn't happy, she was still enamored with him. What her mother called crying, she considered complaining. He was just voicing his opinion with the state of his world.

She could just hear him now. Pausing for a moment, Brigid listened again. Literally, she could hear him. Goose pimples ran up and down her arms. *Has he come back as a ghost?* She didn't move a muscle and listened closer. If he was a ghost, he was still communicating in earthly terms. She heard the faint crying again. It definitely wasn't coming from her room, so he must have been wandering the grounds outside. She got up from the chair as quietly as possible, walked over to her window and peered out.

Jesus, Mary, Joseph. It was a baby, but the child wasn't the ethereal figure she expected to see. It was a real live infant being held in the arms of a person walking briskly towards their barn.

Brigid watched the pair until they entered the structure and were no longer visible. Thoughts raced through her head as she tried to decipher the scene. Most likely the child was being held by his or her mother, but why would any parent be out with a baby in the middle of the night? More importantly, why would they be on the McGinnis property?

The only thing she could come up with was that the woman was in trouble. Maybe the baby was sick or hurt. If that were the case though, why would they walk to a house outside the city limits instead of heading towards town where they'd be more likely to find someone to help them?

Perhaps they were running away. Brigid had heard tales of men who treated their wives poorly. She wasn't personally familiar with such a thing, as her father's conduct towards her mother was above reproach. He never dared say a fractious word to her — out of respect for the fairer sex and with the objective of keeping peace in the household.

Regardless of why the lady and the child were there, as the woman of the house, Brigid knew it was her duty to find them and see if she could be of assistance in some way. That's what her mother would have done if she were capable of it at this point.

Quietly stepping out of the bedroom and closing the door behind her, Brigid took the sconce off the wall in the upstairs hallway and made her way down the curved steps, through the house, and out the back door. While she could have woken one of the male servants to go out with her, she didn't want to put the house into an uproar and frighten the woman away. She must be in need of help or she wouldn't have gone to such lengths to bring her baby to their barn.

Brigid didn't like being outside by herself after dark, but her sense of duty overcame her sense of fear. She doubted the mother presented any danger to her — most likely the woman was just trying to protect her child.

She said a quick Hail Mary before entering the barn. Holding the sconce high, she searched the stalls one by one, swinging the light between them as she went. With a thought to expedite the process, she started calling out softly, "Ma'am, I saw you come in here. Show yourself, I mean you no harm."

A small noise stopped her in her tracks. It was like the sound she heard when she had taken her sisters to see the newborn lambs — a baby suckling. Brigid set the sconce down and tiptoed closer to the last stall. Taking a deep breath to bolster her courage, she poked her head past the wall of the stable.

Sure enough, she had heard correctly. Wedged into the corner of the empty stall, sat a woman with a baby held to her breast. As surreal as the discovery was, there was nothing menacing about the scene. The baby looked content and on the verge of falling asleep. When Brigid stepped near her, the woman pulled the baby in closer to her chest.

Peering down at the female, who couldn't have been any older than she was, Brigid's mouth dropped open. Her skin was slightly darker than her own, but her hair was distinctly different. It was jet black and even though it was pulled back, she could see the wiry texture — the woman was a mulatto. Brigid let out a gasp and regarded the baby closer. It had skin as fair as hers and a head full of stick-straight brown hair. The woman obviously wasn't its mother; she must have been its wet nurse.

But why in the world would a woman be sneaking around in the middle of the night with a child that wasn't her own? The answer struck her like a slap to the face. *Holy God, the child had been kidnapped!*

Chapter XVI

A hearse may be the mode of transportation for people on their way to eternal rest, but Dominic didn't find any relaxation as he rode in one. He felt every rut and rock the cart rolled over. Thank goodness, before he was ensconced in the pine box, he had the foresight to take his overcoat off and put it under his head for a pillow or he would have been nursing two head injuries instead of just one.

Even though Father Barron had poked several holes along each side of the coffin to allow air to enter the space, it was hotter than Hades inside the box. If this was what the underworld felt like, Dominic swore he'd toe the line the rest of his life to avoid that fate.

They stopped twice on the first leg of the journey, when the priest pulled the cart into a wooded area so his passenger could relieve himself, uncramp his legs and have a bite to eat. Each time, Dominic was loath to get back into the confines of the hearse, but it had to be done. It was intolerable traveling at a snail's pace on such a warm early summer day. Sweat pooled under his body as they rolled along.

The vehicle finally came to a halt. Father Barron pulled up to Saint Patrick's Church, where his friend Father Abraham Ryan met him. They were fortunate the man was there because his whereabouts at any particular time were almost impossible to track as of late. Father Barron had relayed Father Ryan's story to Dominic earlier that day. In July of 1863, the priest had been given the heartbreaking news that his brother David had been killed on a battlefield in Monticello, Kentucky, fighting for the Confederate cause. Since that time, Father Ryan had wandered the South in search of the young man's remains. During his travels, he ministered to the sick and dying, whether it was on a battlefield, in a prison, or amongst the civilian population.

Combating bouts of melancholy, Father Ryan began to write poetry to soothe his soul. He became known as the "Poet Priest of the Confederacy." One of his most well-known poems was an ode to his brother titled, "In Memory of My Brother David." The words resounded with the Confederate nation, grieving all their lost youth.

> *Young as the youngest who donned the Gray*
> *True as the truest that wore it —*
> *Brave as the bravest he marched away,*
> *(Hot tears on the cheeks of his mother lay)*
> *Triumphant waved our flag one day,*
> *He fell in the front before it.*

The priest was said to be a relatively young man, so Dominic could understand his sorrow at losing his brother in the prime of his life. It was all too common as the war dragged on. There were women most everywhere dressed in widow's weeds for the obligatory mourning period after the loss of a husband or son. Men sported black armbands and rosettes when a loved one was taken from them. A cloud of death and despair seemed to envelop the entire young nation at a time when it should be experiencing joy, freedom and hope towards the future.

After the cart was pulled into the shed near the rectory, Dominic was finally able to get out. He greeted the priest and excused himself for his disheveled appearance. The cleric was gracious and brushed off his concerns.

That night, Dominic was grateful for a hearty meal prepared by Father Ryan's housekeeper, and for the straw mattress and goose feather pillow he was offered for sleeping accommodations.

They were up early the following morning and on the

road less than an hour after the sun rose. The trip was jarring again but thankfully shorter than the one the day before. Father Barron kept an eye out for roaming companies of soldiers and bandits. For the time being, it looked as though the area north of Atlanta was secure and free from fighting, so they didn't encounter any military personnel. The greater concern was the miscreants roaming the roadways throughout the southern states. Many of these men were deserters, well-trained in the art of war, making their way back to the hovels from whence they came. The unfortunate souls who crossed their paths were undergoing difficult times themselves and more often than not lost what little they had to the brigands.

There was only the need for one stop on this leg of the trip. While they ate a light lunch, Father Barron talked to Dominic to determine in which direction they should go when they got to the city.

"Dominic, it's been a week since you were dealt the head injury. Miss Brigid said things were coming back to you."

"That is true, Father."

"I must know what you remember most recently about your military service. We need to get you back to the Confederate forces. They are hurting for men."

Dominic looked at him calmly, but in his head, he scrambled to stay one step ahead of the conversation. He wanted to prepare the ideal answer to the next question he suspected Father would ask.

Sure enough, out it came.

"Are you ready to go back? If so, we'll have Father O'Reilly make the arrangements. He's in touch with the Confederate officers and has a good handle on where the troops are situated in the area."

"No," said Dominic. As collected as he wanted to sound,

the word came out emphatically.

"No, what?" asked the priest.

"No, sir."

"That's not what I meant. Are you ready to resume your duties with the Confederate Army?"

"No, sir, I'm not," he replied in truth.

"Then shall we bring you to Doctor Burgess' hospital? You will receive stellar care from his staff."

"I would say no to that as well, sir."

"Let me see if I have this straight. You don't feel your injury warrants hospitalization, yet you don't believe you're ready to go back to the front lines. What would you suggest I do with you then? I'd hate to think we made this trip for nothing."

Dominic gathered his thoughts to come up with an acceptable answer. "It's not that I wouldn't benefit from seeing a doctor, but I would imagine the hospitals in the area are overflowing now and I don't want to be a burden to the physician. On the other hand, I'm not sure at this point that I'd know which way was up if I was handed a weapon." He added a tinge of regret for effect.

"Do you think Father O'Reilly would be kind enough to put me up for a couple nights, so I can complete my recuperation?" He continued. "I truly feel I'm on the verge of having full restitution of my memory. Perhaps spending a few days in the presence of God would restore my soul and my wits."

He paused before going in for the kill shot. "I'm doing what I can to listen for direction from the Good Lord. Right now, I feel He's telling me that I'll be of sound mind within a few days. Then I will be able to reintegrate with the troops."

If the religion bit didn't soften up der Priester, nothing would.

Father Barron put his thumb on his chin as if to think about the proposal. Dominic peered at him in anticipation.

After pondering a moment, the man made his declaration.

"That sounds fair enough."

Dominic cleared his throat to cover the sound of the sigh of relief he let out.

"But if you aren't able to return to the front by next weekend, I will instruct Father O'Reilly to have you admitted to the hospital. Do you understand?"

"Yes, sir. Thank you for considering my proposal."

"You're welcome, son. I'll be praying for a complete return of your mental faculties."

"From your lips to God's ears," said Dominic with certainty as he extended his hand forward to shake the priest's hand. He couldn't help but look up to see if the sky was opening above his head. *It doesn't get much worse than fibbing to a priest.*

The two resumed their positions in and on the wagon and got back on the road. When the vehicle at last came to its final stop, Dominic was relieved in more ways than one. So many things could have gone wrong with this plan, but his guardian angel was taking good care of him. At least *he* wasn't holding any grudges. As far as the Big Man Upstairs went, the jury was still out.

All that time alone in the dark casket gave him the chance to think about God and the grand scheme He had for every person's life. There was an expression that stated, "God works in mysterious ways." That had certainly proven to be true in Dominic's life of late.

Getting a severe blow to the head could have been fatal but, not only did he survive, that incident led him to Brigid. For one week in his life, he got to be ministered by as saintly of a woman as he had ever met. She could have handled his situation in a number of different ways that would have been more to her benefit than his, but being the person that she was, she put his welfare first. She took care of his wound, fed him, helped him become literate in her native language, conversed with him and kept him company. Most importantly, they formed a bond that night when they spoke of their pasts. It was a moment he would always remember. He wondered if she felt that same way too.

Like the Blessed Mother, who pronounced her fiat when the Angel Gabriel was sent to her from God, Brigid said yes to helping another human being in need without knowing why but with the knowledge that it was God's will that she do so.

He couldn't help but love her. If it had been acceptable, he would have professed his devotion to her in English, but he knew it wouldn't have been fair to let her know what he was really feeling. Yet, he couldn't keep those words to himself any longer — they had been in his heart from the first moment he laid eyes on her.

But how could they ever be together? He could have feigned continued memory loss and stayed on in Dallas, but their relationship would have been built on a lie.

Another option would have been to abandon his allegiance to the United States of America and join the side of the Confederacy. But that was doubly unacceptable.

With the way the war was turning, he would undoubtedly be putting himself in grave danger — the Rebs were on the run with the Union nipping at their heels. Taking the bigger picture into account, he could not live with himself if he turned traitor. He fought on the side of the Confederate Army once, and he was not going to do it again. Like President Lincoln, Dominic was morally opposed to slavery. He had been raised in a Northern state where slavery was illegal and, more importantly, the practice was condemned by the Catholic Church. *Of course, that didn't seem to bother the Catholics in the slave-holding states who seemed to have found some way to justify the practice.*

He was also in agreement with the president about the need to preserve the union and bring the eleven rebel states back into the fold.

On a more personal note, he knew his best friend Nathan was doing everything he could to get on the right side of the conflict. He would never take up arms again for the Rebels because he did not want to face Nathan across a battlefield. He'd give up his own life before he would take his friend's life.

After Father Barron departed, Dominic would speak to Father O'Reilly in private and see if the man could help him figure out how to get untangled from the web in which he found himself.

Waiting in the parlor for the two priests to finish conducting their business, Dominic considered different ways to broach the topic with Father O'Reilly. Not knowing on which side his loyalty lay, he knew there was only one safe place to talk this out — in the confessional booth.

Chapter XVII

Brigid was familiar with kidnappers, having obtained a copy of the book, *A Narrative of the Life of Mrs. Mary Jemison,* from the library at The Lucy Cobb Institute. It was a true story about a girl who lived with her family in the frontier land of Pennsylvania in the late 1700's. One morning, when she was twelve years old, a raiding party of Shawnee Indians captured Mary, her mother, father and several of her siblings. En route to Fort Duquesne, the Shawnee killed and scalped Mary's parents and brothers and sisters. Mary's life was spared because of her young age. She was adopted by a Seneca family and her name was changed to Pretty Girl. It was quite the harrowing tale.

In her mind, Brigid pictured a kidnapper with a more sinister look. The girl before her didn't fit the mold. But nevertheless, she needed to be turned over to the proper authorities. That baby's parents were probably beside themselves wondering what had become of their child.

Glancing around her, Brigid saw a whip curled up and hung from a peg near the stall. She grabbed it and held it tightly in her right hand. There was no chance she would strike the girl, but she wanted her to know she meant business.

The mulatto's brown eyes widened. Shielding the baby with her body, she looked imploringly at Brigid.

"Please, miss. I beseech you. Do not harm my baby."

Upon hearing those words, Brigid nearly dropped the whip to the barn floor. She couldn't say what shocked her more — the precise English the Negro spoke or the fact that she called the child her own.

She studied her closer, which only added to her bewilderment. The woman wasn't dressed as a slave. As a matter of fact, her frock, although somewhat worn at the collar and cuffs, rivaled any of the day dresses Brigid had hanging in her armoire. Was it perhaps stolen like the child had been?

The scene before her just didn't make any sense. While she stood there pondering, the baby started to fuss. The woman unlatched it from her left side, pulled the fabric of the dress over herself to maintain her modesty and pulled the right shoulder of her dress down. She repositioned the child on the other side to finish its meal.

It was evident that the lady meant no harm to the child and wouldn't be seeking to escape within the next few minutes, so Brigid let her guard down somewhat and returned the whip to its position. She still didn't know what to make of this state of affairs, but she intended to get to the bottom of it.

Bending down to the same level as the woman, she looked her in the eyes and began her examination.

"I don't know why you are in my father's barn, but I intend to find out. You must answer my questions directly and, if I suspect you are lying to me, I will summon the master of the house and you will then be at his mercy." It was a fib, but she felt a venial lie was necessary in this case.

The woman held her gaze.

"Do I make myself clear?"

"Yes, miss. I comprehend precisely."

Again, Brigid was puzzled by the woman's diction. *But just because a person was well-spoken didn't mean they were well-intentioned.* It would take some pointed questions to decipher this situation. She decided to start with the query that was forefront in her mind.

"You look to be a mulatto; am I correct?"

"No, miss. My mother was a mulatto, I am a quadroon."

One-quarter African descent — that explains why her skin is so fair.

"How is it you came to be so articulate?"

The woman tilted her head in a show of pride. "I would imagine the same way you came to be articulate, miss. I was educated."

"Educated? By whom? I'm not aware of any schools for Negro children."

"Nor am I," she replied. "I was tutored by a governess, as were my siblings."

"You do remember what I said about being truthful with me," said Brigid with a stern voice.

"Of course, I do. I am telling the truth."

The whole conversation was surreal. In her entire life, Brigid couldn't recall ever having an actual conversation with a person of a different race. The fact that she was now doing so in a barn, in the middle of the night, with a person who could very well be a criminal made her wonder if she was perhaps dreaming. But she could hear the horses stirring, smell the hay and feel the cool night air on her skin so she knew she was awake.

"You had a governess, so you were raised in a family with some means. Are you a free black then?"

The woman looked reluctant to answer, so Brigid decided to circle back to that line of questioning later.

"You said the child is yours," she continued. "Do you mean the child is in your care? Are you its wet nurse? And if so, why have you taken the child from its mother?"

The woman looked offended. "*I* am his mother. He rightfully belongs to me."

At that moment, the child detached from the woman. Brigid picked up the sconce and held it closer to the baby. If his fair skin and straight hair didn't give his heritage away, the hazel eyes did.

"This child is white," Brigid said emphatically. "You cannot tell me he is yours."

"I beg your pardon, miss, but I can assure you he isn't white. He is, in fact, an octoroon."

Brigid was appalled. "Have you passed yourself off as white in order to marry a white male?" she demanded to know. If this baby was only one-eighth African, then that would mean his father was Caucasian.

The woman set her chin and replied. "I have no husband."

Brigid's jaw dropped. *What kind of scandal was this woman involved in?*

"Then who is the father of this child?"

"I cannot tell you."

"Why on earth not?"

The woman looked to be in a quandary. It took some time before she formulated an answer.

"Josiah is a sweet, innocent child but his father is a wicked human being. I was given to that vile man on his eighteenth birthday, just as my mother had been given to his father when that man became of age." She paused a moment.

"When I discovered I was with child, I did my best to hide it from him as long as I could. He was furious when he found out — as though I were the one at fault. He demanded I get rid of it. A doctor was brought out to the plantation to take care of the problem, but by that time the baby was too far along for him to perform his procedure. Instead, I was given a tonic to drink every night for a week. That was meant to make the baby wither away inside of me."

The woman stared at Brigid as if to gauge her reaction.

Brigid stared back, dumbfounded by what she heard.

"By that time, I was far enough along that the man was disgusted by the look of my body and no longer had the desire to take me to his bed. So I was forced to leave my position in the household as his mother's handmaid and sent to live in the shacks with the field workers. I lied to him and said I took the tonic, but I couldn't do that to my own flesh and blood — regardless who the father was. The baby was born shortly after that, and as you can see, he is perfectly healthy. The man is expecting me to report back to the house tomorrow, but I couldn't abandon Josiah so we left under the cover of darkness earlier tonight."

This was worse than anything Brigid could have imagined. This woman wasn't running off with some other woman's baby — she was an escaped slave.

Chapter XVIII

When Father Barron finally took his leave the next day, Dominic approached Father O'Reilly about seeing him for confession. The man agreed at once. As his role *in persona Christi,* acting as Jesus and as God, he had three main duties — teaching, sanctifying and governing. Hearing confession was the primary sanctifying duty, so Dominic imagined the priest would find a soldier a good candidate for redemption. *Hearing my confession could very well be the highlight of his week.*

There was no need for privacy since Father O'Reilly obviously knew to whom he'd be attending, but the two men followed protocol, walked over to the church proper and proceeded to the confessional. Dominic waited for the priest to enter the middle booth and get settled in and then he took the booth on the left. He shut the gold velvet curtain behind him and lowered himself to the kneeler, which squeaked in protest when he put his full weight upon it.

It had been so long since he had gone to confession that Dominic had to search for the words to begin the process and then translate them in his mind into English.

Father began by inviting him to make the Sign of the Cross.

"*In nomine Patris et Filii et Spiritus Sancti,*" said Dominic in unison with the priest. He thought a little more and then began. "Bless me Father, for I have sinned. It's been ten..." he paused to do the math in his head, "make that eleven years since my last confession."

"Oh me goodness," said the reverend in his Irish brogue. "It's a good thing ye've come to see me today, I'm sure ye've got a lot on yer mind."

"You could say that, Father." *That would be an understatement, if I ever heard one.* But Dominic truly did want to make a good confession. He soon would be back on the battlefield and if things didn't turn out well, this could be his last chance to be absolved of his sins. He didn't want to spend all of eternity in purgatory. There was no guarantee there'd be anyone praying for his release. The thought of spending perpetuity wandering around as a lost soul was a glum one.

"Let's start with an examination of conscience, shall we, son, perhaps with the Ten Commandments."

Dominic wasn't expecting a trick question. He could barely remember the Ten Commandments when his mother first drilled them into his head as a youngster — he'd be lucky to recall half of them now when he was put on the spot.

"It's been a while, Father. Can you refresh me on those?"

"Certainly. Thou shall have no other gods before Me. Thou shall not make idols. Thou shall not take the name of the Lord your God in vain. Remember the Sabbath day, to keep it holy. Honor your father and mother. Thou shall not murder. Thou shall not commit adultery. Thou shall not steal. Thou shall not bear false witness against your neighbor. Thou shall not covet."

While the man was speaking, Dominic was ticking each item off from a list in his head. *Thou shall have no other gods before Me. Thou shall not make idols.* As far as he knew, there wasn't any other God so nothing to report there.

Thou shall not take the name of the Lord your God in vain. That one needed to go on the list. He learned to cuss from the two young rascals he lived with when his parents died. After his run-in with Frau Charity, he never used that one particular swear word again, but cursing was a hard habit to break. Things had a tendency to go awry when working the land and raising animals and crops. He had been known to voice his displeasure in colorful language from time to time.

Remember the Sabbath day, to keep it holy. This one wasn't quite as cut and dried. Dominic always knew which day of the week it was so, technically, he remembered the Sabbath, but he hadn't attended Mass in years. For the most part, there were no churches available to him when he was on the farms and ranches plying his trade. But he admitted some opportunities had availed themselves for him to get to church, but for whatever reason he chose not to take advantage of them.

Honor thy father and mother. His score was pretty good in that column when it came to his *Mutter*. He had been very close to her. She not only instructed him on his school subjects, but taught him about their faith, instilled in him a respect for all living beings, and demonstrated the strength and determination of which women are capable.

His relationship with his *Vater* was a bit more complicated. The man taught him the value of hard work, determination, and deference for the land and the forces which prevailed upon it. But he was a strict taskmaster and demanded perfection from his son even at an early age. Perhaps Dominic deserved the whippings he received every so often — admittedly he was belligerent at times. It was hard to understand why his father had him working his fingers to the bone when other children his age were allowed to have fun and play. The two of them butted heads quite a bit when Dominic entered his teen years.

It was painful thinking back on their last encounter — the day he was picking rocks from the field with his *Mutter* before the fire started. Certain his *Vater* overworked him, Dominic grumbled as he went about the backbreaking work. The last words he spoke to the man had been less than charitable, and they haunted him ever since. As an adult he could see how hard the man worked and how he was trying to instill solid values into his son. Johann Warner was gruff and stern, but he made Dominic the man he was today. *I regret I will never be able to thank him in person.* The next best thing he could do was live out a life that would make his *Vater* proud.

Thou shall not murder. Dominic made the assumption that taking someone's life during a time of war was justifiable homicide, so he moved onto the next item.

Thou shall not commit adultery. Even if he had thoughts of doing such a thing, the women on the frontier were few and far between. The only married woman he interacted with was Maria, Eduardo's wife. With her rotund figure, sweet disposition, and continually invoking *Ave Maria* for the health and protection of everyone on the ranch, she was like a grandmother to him.

Thou shall not steal. Other than taking some fruit from the trees or vegetables out of a field here and there to keep from starving when he was between jobs, Dominic couldn't think of anything of great consequence, but he would mention that to Father, just in case. *Shoot, there was that coat he took when he left Frau Charity's farm.* He'd have to add that to the list.

Thou shall not bear false witness against your neighbor. He rolled his eyes up to the left, trying to think of anything, but nothing came to mind.

Thou shall not covet. There was no way around this one. Dominic was coveting something all right, or should he say, someone. Immediately the picture of Brigid came to mind. As much as he wanted her, she belonged to her father and once he relinquished his dominion over her, she would be part of a religious order. Coveting something that belonged to God would be a mortal sin — there was no doubt about it.

It was a good thing he got to Father O'Reilly when he did.

Dominic began his confession, deciding to tackle the biggest transgression first.

"Father, I didn't hear you mention it on the list, but I've been doing my share of lying lately."

"To whom have ye spoken mistruths?" the priest inquired.

"In the past week, it would be Father Barron, a young lady named Brigid McGinnis, and you."

"Hmmm...that's quite an impressive list. Explain yerself."

"I know Father Barron told you my story. While it's true I was engaged in a confrontation on the battlefield and a blow to the head took my memory from me, the full effects were short-lived. I was actually completely recovered within forty-eight hours of meeting Miss McGinnis, whose yard I landed in after the attack. I've been covering up the truth, not only from her, but from both Father Barron and you as well."

"I see," said Father O'Reilly. "What would cause ye to perpetuate that misconception, son?"

"Well, that leads me to the next lie I've been living these past several months. I may be wearing a Confederate uniform, but I'm not a Rebel — I'm a Unionist."

"Are ye telling me yer a double agent for the Union Army? That would be a serious admission."

"Not exactly, Father. That does sound intriguing, but my story isn't quite as glamorous. The fact is, I was conscripted against my will to fight for the Confederate States of America. When the opportunity is afforded to me, I plan to defect to the side of the Union. That's where I'm hoping you will step in."

"Ye understand, son, that I will not go against me own conscience, no matter what the circumstance."

"Absolutely, Father. I would not ask you to do something unethical. Let's get back to that in a moment. We'll tackle one sin at a time."

A sigh came from the other side of the curtain.

He continued, "The young lady I mentioned — she has a good heart and took care of me after our initial encounter. She put herself at risk keeping me hidden in her house while I was recovering. I pray her soul isn't in jeopardy for harboring me. When I regained my memory, I kept it from her because I wanted more time in her presence and more time to figure out my course of action."

Dominic paused. "I must confess that I do covet her. But don't get me wrong, Father. My intentions towards her are honorable — I have a deep affection for her and would ask her father's permission to court her if circumstances were different."

It was quiet on the other side of the veil, as if the priest were sorting through everything he had just heard.

"Let me see if I have this straight. Ye are a Confederate soldier, not by choice, but by circumstance. A head injury on the field caused ye te temporarily lose yer memory. A young lass took ye into her home te nurse ye back to health. In that process, ye developed feelings fer her. Upon regaining yer memory, ye neglected to tell her so ye could extend yer time with her and presumably not alert her to the fact that ye weren't the Confederate soldier she presumed ye to be. Do I have that correct?"

"Basically, yes, sir."

"Ye still have a chance to set things right. I can help ye join up with a Union regiment in the area so ye can follow yer conscience on that front. If General Sherman has his way, the war will be coming to a conclusion within a few months. Assuming ye survive, when yer dismissed from service, go find her and follow courting protocol. At that point, we would hope the states will be on one side again and whether a soldier wore the blue or the gray, they'd all be united as brothers in Christ — so your allegiance during the conflict should have no bearing on your future with this woman."

He paused as if to let Dominic consider his plan. "What think ye of that?"

"I think the arrangement has merit but there is one hitch — Miss McGinnis is planning on taking vows with a religious order."

While Dominic could not see the man on the other side of the curtain, he could just picture him with his mouth agape. It took nearly a minute before he replied.

"Sweet Lord Jesus. I'm not sure there be enough Hail Marys and Our Fathers te cover this penance."

Chapter XIX

Brigid was in a quandary. Her father would disown her if he knew she was talking to a Negro, but if he ever found out she was harboring a slave on their property, there truly would be hell to pay. If that prospect wasn't enough to give her heart palpitations, she was well aware that Mr. McGinnis wasn't the only man in Georgia who abhorred fugitives. Bounty hunters were greedy for money and human flesh. She recalled the conversation she had with Stewart and chills ran down her spine. They were paid not only to capture escaped slaves but their white sympathizers as well.

There was talk that abolitionists had set up something referred to as the Underground Railroad to help Negroes escape their bonds of enslavement. Businesses and homes open to harboring fugitive slaves were known as depots and were run by stationmasters. Conductors moved the slaves from one station to the next until the runaways were safely deposited in the far northern states or Canada where they legally could not be repossessed by their owners. Men like Stewart were determined to shut the railroad down.

While Brigid had sympathy for the plight of the slaves, she didn't want to get involved with the issue. Slavery was one of those topics that her father considered men's business, and that was fine by her. Besides, slaveholding was part and parcel of life in the Southern states, especially for the plantation owners and people in her father's circle of friends. Slaves did the work white people didn't want to do, and she imagined the economy in the South would suffer mightily without that labor force.

She did her best not to think about it. Even though intrinsically the practice didn't feel right to her, she chose to turn a blind eye to it as much as she could. It really was of no concern to her anyhow — her father didn't own any slaves. Their servants worked for them of their own volition. The men and women weren't mistreated and had adequate provisions, so employment with the McGinnis family was obviously satisfactory for them.

Disregarding the topic of slavery had been easy enough when the slaves were someone else's business, but as Brigid stood face-to-face with one, it was hard to ignore. She had no intention of turning the woman in — she presumed both the mother and the child would face dire circumstances if they were returned to their owner. It would bother her conscience something awful if anything happened to them because of her.

That being said, she did not want to become ensnared in this situation and have word get out that an escaped slave had been found on their property. The McGinnis family would never be able to live that impropriety down. Brigid would have to figure out a way to get the woman to depart from their land as soon as possible.

With that in mind, she turned towards the female to issue orders for the pair to leave their barn. "Miss, um. What name do you go by?"

The woman looked at her warily. "I'd prefer not to reveal that if you don't mind, not until I discover your true character."

Character? Brigid couldn't believe the woman had the audacity to judge her. *How dare she question my character when she's the one sneaking around on private property!*

"Listen, missy. I will have you know that my character is above reproach. Our family is well respected in this town and, personally, I intend to say vows to the Church later this year. So I'd appreciate it if you didn't question my morals."

"Yes, miss," she said in a less-than-conciliatory tone.

Brigid wasn't sure how to take the woman. On one hand she admired her for her pluckiness but, on the other hand, she was a bit offended because the quadroon wasn't acquiescing to a person who obviously outranked her on the scale of human hierarchy.

She would have to give that further thought some other time. Even though her father said Negroes were less than human — three-fifths to be exact — this woman seemed very self-assured, something Brigid wished she could say about herself. *Perhaps the government calculations were off?*

Getting back on track, she continued, willing herself to sound as certain as her adversary did. "Now that we have that settled, let me reassure you, even though as a dutiful citizen I should turn you over to the proper authorities, I have decided to let you go. You may take a few minutes to attend to your child but then I would ask that you vacate this building."

The woman seemed intent on maintaining her composed expression, but relief was evident on her face. "Thank you, miss. I truly am grateful for your leniency."

"You may call me Miss Brigid, if you'd care to. And your name is?"

"Alice."

"Well, it was a pleasure getting to know you, Alice, but I assume you'd like to put some distance between yourself and this town before the sun rises, so we should say our adieus."

A look of uncertainty crossed the woman's face.

"*Adieu.* That means good-bye in French."

"*Je comprends,*" said the woman haughtily.

Brigid squinted her eyes to stop them from rolling. "Is there something else wrong? Am I not being generous enough with your fate?"

"You truly are, Miss Brigid, but it's a bit more complicated than that."

"How's that?"

She looked Brigid straight in the eye. "It isn't just me."

"Obviously, I know you have the baby to think of."

"It's not just Josiah either. It's the others."

"What others?" questioned Brigid with a note of alarm in her voice.

"It's my brother and his intended and their son," Alice replied, keeping her voice low.

"What about them?"

"They're here too," she said.

Brigid put her hand to her chest, backed against the rough barn wall and looked around wildly.

"In here?"

"No, miss. In the root cellar."

"Root cellar? *Our* root cellar?" Brigid asked in disbelief.

Seeing the girl nodding in affirmation, the next question seemed an obvious one.

"What are they doing there?"

"It's a depot," the lady answered in a hushed tone.

Brigid's head grew light and stars formed in front of her eyes. *A depot? Was she referring to the Underground Railroad?* It wasn't possible. How could something so devious be happening in their house beneath the nose of her father, an esteemed member of President Davis' cabinet and a staunch defender of the rights of the slave-holding states?

Then the thought hit her — this wasn't happening under her father's nose; this was happening under her nose when he was in Virginia performing his duties for the

Confederacy. Someone —privy to her father's schedule —
must be informing the conductors of when their house was
a safe haven. The only person she could think of who
followed her father's schedule that closely was Mr. Mason.
Could he possibly be involved with this subterfuge?

Would he dare to create a depot on the McGinnis
property? That *could* explain the noises she heard at night
when her father was out of town. Somebody was letting the
fugitives into their root cellar. But the door was padlocked,
so only someone with a key would have the ability to do that.
It wasn't her mother, her little sisters or herself. Some
member of their household staff must be helping conduct
these human beings out of Georgia by using their house as
a station. Was someone perhaps in cahoots with Mr.
Mason? But why would anyone show such disloyalty to such
a fair employer as her father?

This was more information than Brigid could digest at
the moment. By hearing Alice's admission, she would be
implicating herself in this whole ordeal if she didn't turn
them all in at once.

Alice must have guessed where her thoughts were going
because she looked up at Brigid with pleading eyes.

"Please, Miss Brigid, have compassion on my family. If
you knew the despicable conditions all the colored folks
endure on the plantation, you would have pity on us. Shall I
show you the scars on my back from being whipped by my
master for his own sadistic satisfaction?"

The blood drained from Brigid's face. She would take the
woman at her word — she had no need to see that.

"You say you're a female of principles and that you
intend to devote your life to the Church," continued Alice.
"Are you not familiar with First Corinthians, chapter seven,
verses twenty-two and twenty-three? 'You see, anyone who

was called in the Lord while a slave, is a freeman of the Lord; and in the same way, anyone who was free when called, is a slave of Christ. You have been bought at a price; do not be slaves now to any human being.'"

As humbling as it was to admit, Brigid wasn't familiar with that Bible passage. Unlike her Fundamentalist acquaintances, she didn't actually know any Bible passages by heart. Of course, the McGinnis family kept their Bible in the parlor, but no one actually ever read it. It was mostly used to record births and deaths and for pressing an occasional wildflower. Nonetheless, the words hit Brigid squarely; she could hardly take a breath in.

"We don't want to get you embroiled in this situation, Miss Brigid, but I'm pleading for your help. My nephew is only a few months old, and something isn't right with him. His breathing is impaired, and we don't know if he can tolerate the damp night air. We're just requesting a couple of days for him to recuperate before we resume our journey."

All Brigid could think of when she heard about the child was her own baby brother. She was torn apart when he died, and the last thing she wanted to do was to put Alice's family through that same ordeal.

Think, think, think..., Brigid commanded herself.

It would just be a few days and, God willing, this would be the end of it. She'd find out which servant was involved in this business and send him or her packing.

"You may stay, but as soon as the baby's health is stabilized, you must leave at once."

Relief washed over Alice's face and she tilted her head up toward the barn roof as if thanking the heavens. With the baby balanced in one arm, she got up and followed Brigid as she proceeded towards the barn door.

Stopping before they exited, Brigid looked behind her at Alice. "I will do what I can to make you comfortable for the remainder of your stay. The members of your party are hungry and thirsty, I would imagine. I'll fetch some libations and put together a poultice to rub on the baby's chest to help clear his lungs. Now get yourself back into the root cellar. I'll be down there shortly."

The woman did as she was told, and Brigid went into the house to gather the provisions. She wrapped everything in a cloth and grabbed the copper pitcher she had most recently filled for Dominic. Then she quietly left the kitchen and, visibly shaking, walked outside to the root cellar door. She let herself in. Alice, still clutching her baby, sat beside another woman holding an older baby and the man she assumed was Alice's brother. The male was a bit taller than Dominic and as solid as a tree trunk. The definition of every muscle was visible on his arms. He was barrel-chested with a thick neck. Under any other circumstance, she would have been quite intimidated by the man. But she could see the look of concern on his face as she reached for his child. The woman reluctantly handed the baby to her — they were probably just as anxious as she was.

Brigid set the pitcher and the cloth on a shelf and unwrapped the fabric to get the poultice. Lifting the baby's gown, she slowly rubbed the concoction on his chest. His skin was as smooth as any baby's, but the contrast in their skin tones was remarkable. Brigid's fingers trembled as she went about her ministrations. The sensation must have been soothing to the child as he gave her a big toothless grin. Brigid couldn't help but smile back. He reminded her so much of Baby John. Tears clouded her eyes.

Satisfied with her work, she lowered the gown and handed the infant to his mother. The woman nodded her thanks. Alice turned a hand up to introduce the occupants of the space, but Brigid shushed her. The last thing she wanted was to learn their names and get more entangled in the situation — she was in far enough as it was.

With her tasks finished, Brigid turned and walked up the steps, slowly shut the door behind her and went back into the house. Holding the copper pitcher again made her think of Dominic. As much as she tried to push those thoughts to the back of her mind, they kept creeping forward like a fog engulfing the countryside on a moist, cool summer night.

She should have headed to bed but her feet, unbidden, took her back to her father's study. She grabbed the wall sconce, cracked open the door, and slipped into the room, shutting the door behind her. Dominic had been gone for forty-eight hours, yet she could still feel his presence in the room. She smoothed the fabric on the fainting sofa where he had slept. Holding the small pillow to her face, she inhaled his aroma — it was masculine with a hint of leather and outdoors. It was nothing less than intoxicating.

Would he be pleased with her for showing the gumption to handle the situation laid out before her that evening? She liked to think that he would have been.

Glancing at the bookshelf, she thought back to when she sat next to him on the rug and taught him how to sound out words in English. She walked to the shelf and took hold of the book that was slightly out of alignment from the other tomes. *Great Expectations. Something of which I have none*, she thought gloomily. It was too bad they hadn't had time to finish the book. That thought inspired her to flip through the pages to see how much was left to read. As she did, a slip of paper fell out of the book.

It floated to the floor and Brigid bent over to pick it up. Her father's neat script on what looked to be a receipt. There was only one item listed and the charge was five hundred and fifty dollars. Squinting to decipher the small, tidy script,

Brigid read the description and then, not believing her eyes, read it again. It wasn't a purchase record for building supplies or farm goods — it was a receipt for a human being, identified by markings on its body.

A slave acquisition? Brigid's head started to buzz and the words blurred before her eyes. But the date at the top of the ledger was clear — the first day of February in the year of the Lord 1862. The transaction was made two years ago on Brigid's fifteenth birthday.

That was the day Tilly came to work for their family as Brigid's handmaid. But she wasn't a slave — or was she? Had she been purchased by Mr. McGinnis? Six people were on staff at their house. Had her father lied to her and told her they were paid servants when, in actuality, they were slaves? Were they here against their will?

That could explain a lot of things, such as why they had such a low turnover of help, why the children were forbidden from interacting with the staff, and why the servants never left the grounds unless they were performing assigned duties for the McGinnis family. Except for Mr. Mason, who came and went as he pleased when he wasn't attending to Mr. McGinnis' needs. Perhaps he actually was a free black. Maybe he was the conductor directing runaway slaves to their property. Had he coerced the other staff members to be operatives as well? Someone was obviously letting those people into their root cellar.

Brigid didn't know what to make of the situation. She just needed to put the receipt back where she found it, return the book to the shelf, and get herself up to her room, where she could sort things through her mind.

Quickly climbing the curved stairs to the second floor, she kept close to the wall where the wood was less wont to creak. The bed looked inviting when she crossed the threshold into her room, but there was no time for sleeping now. Sinking into the Empire chair, she leaned back against a pillow. All she could do was stare straight ahead as she went over what she had just discovered. It was too much to absorb, so her mind shut down. After a moment she drifted off to sleep.

Somewhere beyond her window, a noise entered her consciousness. It was the cadence of a horse pulling a buggy into their drive. Brigid bolted up, instantly wide awake. She would know that sound anywhere. *Good Gracious Lord,* her father was home.

Chapter XX

For a man of the cloth, it sounded like Father O'Reilly had quite a few contacts in the secular world. Dominic was still on his knees in penance when the priest excused himself. He exited through the large carved doors of the church and left the grounds to meet with some acquaintances who had knowledge of the warfront.

Once the priest was out of sight, Dominic was tempted to do an abbreviated penance — perhaps skip a few Hail Marys or Our Fathers. But he had things he needed to atone for and if he didn't take care of this now, Lord only knew when the next chance would avail itself. Realizing he would soon be going back to the battle lines, it seemed prudent to stay in the Lord's good graces. Like most men in the throes of war, he knew any moment could be his last and he'd much rather meet Saint Peter at the Pearly Gates than encounter his nemesis at the entrance to Hades.

By the time he rose from the kneeler, he had to shake his legs to get the feeling back in his feet. Thinking over what he had confessed to Father O'Reilly, Dominic tried to determine if any one of the offenses he had enumerated were mortal sins. He dug through his memory banks, trying to recall the catechism he learned from his *Mutter* — she had taught him the difference between mortal and venial sins.

It took a few moments but it finally came back to him. For a sin to be mortal, it must meet three conditions — it must be a sin of grave matter, committed with full knowledge of the sinner, and committed with deliberate consent of the sinner.

Grave matter? Every one of the Ten Commandments

concerned a grave matter — off the top of his head he knew he had broken at least four of them. It was a wonder he got off his knees as quickly as he had.

But reciting prayers was just one aspect of penance. The other part was making reparation for the transgressions committed. Father was quite emphatic that Dominic find a way to apologize to Brigid for leading her astray. *Easier said than done.* While he now was progressing at reading English, his writing skills in that language were minimal — it would take him forever and a day to pen a comprehensible note. He could ask the priest to transcribe a missive for him, but it would be next to impossible to deliver a letter to Brigid without someone in her family finding out. The McGinnis house would be abuzz if anyone discovered that Brigid had received correspondence from a soldier.

He certainly didn't want to put her in that position. But, as far as apologizing in person, he could not imagine how to make that happen. Getting to Atlanta had been a huge undertaking, and he couldn't think of any plausible way to return to Dallas in the middle of a war to make amends. Perhaps after the hostilities were over he would be able to find out which religious order she joined, get himself to the motherhouse and beg her pardon. But for the time being, there wasn't much he could do.

Now he just needed to be patient and wait for Father to return. Dominic walked down the aisle of the Church of the Immaculate Conception. The building itself was a simple wooden structure but the stained-glass windows were remarkable — each one depicted a scene from the New Testament of the Bible, beginning with the Blessed Mother being visited by the angel Gabriel announcing God's plan for her.

Between each window was a small plaster figurine situated on a wooden shelf representing a Station of the

Cross. In the front of the church stood life-sized statues of Saint Joseph the Worker and his wife Mary, holding their infant son, Jesus.

Dominic paused before the figure of Saint Joseph. He felt a kinship with the man who worked with his hands his whole life. *Just like me.* Spontaneously, he dropped to one knee and prayed aloud.

"Blessed Saint Joseph, I come before you, a humble and sinful man, asking for your intercession on my behalf. I'm requesting protection when I go back into battle and also that this war will conclude soon. If my friend Nathan is still living, I implore your intercession for his continued safety as well."

It was hard to believe that it wasn't much more than a month ago that he and Nathan were together on their ranch. Now that his memory was completely restored, the events that led up to the blow upon his head came rushing back to him.

After they received their conscription notices, they were shipped with the rest of the men rounded up in their region to join the 53rd Tennessee Infantry. All the new recruits were sworn in as privates, but Nathan with his stellar marksmanship skills caught the attention of a commanding officer and was promoted to the rank of corporal within a week.

With his competitive nature, he couldn't let Nathan outrank him, so one day he approached a sergeant and made him a proposition. If the gentleman would be kind enough to act as judge, he and Nathan would have a shooting contest. They would carve a target into a tree about fifty yards outside of camp. If he shot closer to the bull's-eye than Nathan, then he would be promoted to corporal. If Nathan outshot him, then he would take on the sergeant's menial tasks for a week.

The man agreed. The younger soldiers were each allowed three shots at the target. Two of his shots ended up being closer to the center spot than Nathan's, so he was declared the winner and got another set of chevrons to sew onto his sleeves.

On the twenty-fourth day of May, 1864, the two corporals had their first taste of war. Before the engagement, he and Nathan made a vow to do whatever it took to escape the Confederate Army and make their way to a Union camp. If they got separated, they were to meet back at Heavenly Vista Ranch when they were discharged from service.

Things didn't turn out as either of them had planned. General Joseph E. Johnston, commander of the Confederate forces in Georgia, formed a defensive line along the south side of Pumpkinvine Creek. His Union counterpart, Major General William T. Sherman, became aware of the movement and a series of skirmishes began. Johnston's army, of which the 53rd Tennessee was a part, fell back to the Dallas area to entrench. Sherman's army tested the Rebel line. That's when fate stepped in.

Both he and Nathan were targeting Union soldiers with their pistols, shooting and reloading as quickly as they could. Nathan was peering around the left side of a tree, measuring up his next shot, and he was a few yards behind him getting more shot ready for his pistol. Out of the corner of his eye, he glimpsed a Union soldier coming up behind Nathan. The man must have been out of ammunition as he had his weapon above his head, looking to strike Nathan while his attention was focused on the target before him. Seeing the event unfolding, he dropped his gun and burst towards the soldier. A moment before he was set to tackle him, the soldier turned and brought the butt of his gun down on Dominic's temple.

The blow stunned him, but the momentum pushed him forward and he toppled the man onto the blade of a knife wedged between the roots of the tree. The man was impaled by the steel and instantaneously went limp. In revulsion, he rolled off the man's body and then staggered to the tree to pull himself up. Looking around, he couldn't see Nathan anywhere. Being unarmed and barely able to see through the blood running into his eyes, instinct made him turn away from the fight and weave through the trees to get away. The first conscious thought he was aware of came to him when he was lying in the yard next to the McGinnis house.

Dominic glanced over his shoulder to be sure no one was in the sanctuary with him. He shut his eyes and continued. "There's strength in numbers, Saint Joseph, so if you don't mind passing this along to Saint Jude, I have a request. You took the Virgin Mary as your wife, when most everyone probably advised you not to, so if there is any way this can be worked out in my favor, I would like to be able to ask Brigid for her hand in marriage."

He opened one eye and checked to see if a stray bolt of lightning was headed in his direction. Seeing no flashing illumination, he bowed his head in reverence, said "*Danke,*" made the Sign of the Cross, and then backed away from the image of the good saint.

Taking a seat in a pew, Dominic waited for Father O'Reilly to return. An hour or so later he heard the large wooden double doors being opened. He turned and saw the priest hurrying up the aisle towards his seat.

"I've got good news fer ye," said the man.

That might be one way to look at it, thought Dominic as he anticipated what he was about to hear.

Father O'Reilly shared what he learned from his

emissary. On the 28th of May, General William J. Hardee tried probing the Union defensive line in Dallas, which was held by General John Alexander Logan's Army of the Tennessee. The Rebels were repulsed and in the process suffered high casualties. *That explained the gunfire I heard when I was at the McGinnis house last week.*

According to the priest, Sherman had plans to flank Johnston from the south and push him northeast toward the Atlanta-Chattanooga Railroad. Union troops were just outside of Atlanta, preparing for the surge.

Father O'Reilly made arrangements to connect Dominic with the nearest Federal regiment.

Whether it was an ironic circumstance or a sign of good fortune, the priest announced that within hours Dominic would be pleading his oath of allegiance to the Union Army, 2nd Brigade, 2nd Division, XIV Corps — the 78th Illinois Volunteer Infantry Regiment.

Chapter XXI

Brigid jumped from her bed and ran straight to her bedroom door. She needed to intercept her father before he got to the house. Hopefully, the fugitives in the root cellar would hear her greeting him and be extra vigilant to avoid detection.

She scurried down the steps, ran through the house to the back door and was out in the yard before her father's buggy came to a halt. The man seated on the velvet cushion saw his daughter through the small square window and nodded his head to acknowledge her.

"Father, it's so wonderful that you're back," said Brigid when the vehicle came to a halt, enunciating each word in a voice louder than her usual tone.

Mr. McGinnis looked at her quizzically. She noticed Mr. Mason shifting his eyes towards her as well.

"I'm certainly glad to see you too, my daughter, but is there some reason you're speaking so loudly? You might not only awaken the household but the dead as well."

"My apologies, sir. I'm just excited to see you," she said in a more subdued tone.

"I can imagine you're anxious to hear what news I bring you about your vocation. But it certainly can wait until morning," he said as his manservant helped him out of the vehicle.

Her father was correct about her being anxious, but he would never have imagined what was really troubling her. The last thing on her mind right now was the nunnery. It was only the first week of June — she saw no reason to put too much thought to that since she wouldn't be entering the convent until at least autumn.

It soon became apparent that they weren't on the same

timeline. "But, since you're here, I'll fill you in." Once Mr. Mason stepped away allowing them to converse in private, her father continued. "I had a considerable amount of work to do for President Davis, but I made time to research appropriate religious orders for you. I've come up with the ideal situation."

Brigid's eyes widened as she waited to hear his proclamation.

"As you may recall, I was looking for an order that is well-established, has an impeccable reputation, and yet is a reasonable distance from here. But I also sought out an organization that performed acts of charity, like St. Brigid of Kildare, in whose honor you were named."

He proceeded to pull a piece of paper out of the jacket of his overcoat. After meticulously unbending each fold, he scanned it, then glanced down at his daughter. "In my research, I learned about Catherine McAuley, an Irish Catholic laywoman, who in the early part of this century, recognized the many needs of poor people in Ireland. She was determined that she and other women like her could make a difference in the lives of those unfortunates. So she spent her inheritance to open a house of mercy in Dublin in 1827 to shelter and educate women and girls. While she originally intended to assemble a lay corps of Catholic social workers, she was instructed by the Archbishop of Dublin to establish a religious congregation."

He paused and looked again at the paper. "In 1831, she and two companions became the first Sisters of Mercy. Nuns from their order arrived in the United States in 1843. Their enthusiasm for ministering to the sick and poor brought so many new members that ten years ago they established communities in New York City, Chicago, San Francisco and Little Rock. With the war continuing on, the good sisters felt it necessary to expand their operations into

Georgia, so they opened a community in Cartersville. As you know, that's less than a day's ride from here."

His knowledge of the Sisters of Mercy was admirable; Brigid knew he had done his due diligence researching, as he was wont to do with any major decision for his business or family.

"Just so you're aware, the process of becoming a sister takes several years. During that time, you and the community will mutually discern whether God is calling you to be a sister. You will pray, you will learn, you will study theology and minister alongside the other women."

"Yes, Father." It was the only thing Brigid could think to say. Even though they had discussed this matter for more than a year, it didn't seem real until now. *If only Dominic hadn't appeared in my life,* she thought, *I wouldn't find myself in the dilemma I'm now facing.*

Regardless, she would have at least two months to shake the thoughts of that handsome soldier out of her head before she left for the convent.

Or so she thought.

"I want you to go to bed now," her father said in a somewhat stern voice. "Tomorrow you will pack your things. The following morning Jeremiah will drive you to Cartersville. Fate is on our side; you'll be able to enroll immediately. The summer term begins next week."

Brigid was thankful that the darkness hid the look of astonishment on her face. Her father had no idea what thoughts were racing through her head. It would be of little interest to him anyhow. Once his mind was made up on a topic, there was no changing course.

"Off you go, young lady. I need to get some sleep myself, so let's not dillydally out here anymore and chance waking the girls. They'd be bright-eyed and bushy-tailed, ready to start their antics for the day. I could use some peace and quiet for a few hours."

Obedient as she always was, Brigid did an about-face and walked back into the house and up to her room. Her father may have been looking forward to sleeping, but she knew that would not be possible for her. She needed to cobble together a plan to get Alice and her family out of the root cellar by the time she left. God forbid her father stumble across them.

Times like these made Brigid wish she was less like Saint Brigid and more like her classmates at the Lucy Cobb Institute. They seemed only to think about themselves. *Why must I be so compassionate?* Maybe this was a sign that the religious life would suit her — she barely even knew those people hiding in the root cellar, yet she felt compelled to help them.

But how exactly would she do that? They could only leave the house under the cover of darkness, so that left one night for them to make their escape. She doubted the baby would be recovered from his illness that quickly.

Two years ago, her baby brother had left his earthly bonds and he was now a saint up in heaven. She would ask his intercession to help her come up with a plan. *Saint John Thaddeus McGinnis II,* she began to pray, *this is your sister Brigid. I miss you, but I trust you are enjoying your heavenly realm. I have a favor to ask of you. If it wouldn't be too much bother, could you petition our Lord on my behalf? Please ask him to show me the way to proceed with this situation. What would be the safest way to move Alice and her family on to their next destination so they can continue their flight north?*

With a sense of anticipation, Brigid sat on her bed, not moving a muscle, waiting for a verbal answer. She heard nothing but in time a picture formed in her head. It was the coach stored in the barn their family used when they all traveled together. There was space in the vehicle for several trunks — it was much roomier than the Brougham her father used on his trips to and from Virginia.

She wouldn't need trunks full of clothes if she became a sister, but the chests could hold things other than finery. In fact, if she was estimating correctly, each one was large enough to fit a full-grown adult if they scrunched down.

That was how she could get the Negro family off their property and onto their next stop. Each adult could ensconce themselves away inside one of the trunks and the trunks could be loaded onto the coach. She would need to take Jeremiah into her confidences since she didn't have the ability to load the trunks herself. She prayed he would be amenable to the idea. Hopefully, a few coins most certainly would have him seeing her way.

It was a bit troublesome because Brigid didn't want to put Jeremiah's life at risk, but she wasn't asking him to do something she wouldn't do — her own neck was on the line.

Chapter XXII

Strolling into a Union camp dressed in gray trousers and a gray jacket with a Confederate insignia sewed onto one's lapel would be foolhardy. It seemed to make sentries jumpy when their sworn enemies moseyed onto their property uninvited. *And there's nothing worse than a jittery sentry with a loaded gun.*

Knowing that, Father O'Reilly scrounged up some civilian clothes for Dominic to put on before they left to find where the Union Army 78th Illinois Volunteer Infantry Regiment was holed up.

Securing clothes had been one thing, deciding what story to give the guards when they arrived in camp was another. It was especially difficult when dealing with a priest because lying didn't seem to come as easily to him as it did to those folks who weren't of the cloth.

Father O'Reilly's first impulse was to tell the plain, simple truth. It sounded good in theory, but Dominic wasn't sure how it would go over with the Union officers. There was so much espionage going on at this point in the war that it would seem highly suspicious for a corporal in the Confederate Army to have a change of heart and want to join the Union ranks. It wasn't like a game of baseball — switching teams during a war was a bit more complicated.

So Dominic was charged with coming up with a plausible tale that in essence was the truth yet omitted any incriminating facts about himself. It would be easy enough to start with the story about how he was raised in Illinois but had been ranching in Texas the last several years. He would tell them about how he and his business partner were minding their own beeswax, to not let on they were Union sympathizers and how that had worked just fine for the first few years, seeing as how they were supplying Confederate troops with food.

That was the part where it got tricky. Dominic didn't want to mention the detail about actually being conscripted by the Reb Army. He considered saying that he and Nathan heard about the conscription act, *which they had*, and the last thing they wanted to do, *which was true*, was to fight on the side of Jeff Davis. The intention, *which it was*, had been for them to make their way to a Union camp and volunteer their services to President Abraham Lincoln and the United States of America.

If asked about Nathan, Dominic would say there had been an incident and only one of them had been able to continue on. Someone had told him about Father O'Reilly, and the priest was able to determine which Union camp was closest to The Church of the Immaculate Conception and, by chance, it was the Illinois regiment.

Thankfully, Father O'Reilly agreed to that version of the story, so the two men practiced it several times as they rode together on the rectory horse to the encampment outside the city. They decided to use the mare and no buggy because it would be quicker. Since most of the guards were familiar with the priest, the pair should be able to make their way inside the camp without any fuss.

The situation would truly be ideal if there was someone in the 78th Illinois who recognized him and could corroborate his identity. He had certainly worked on his share of farms and ranches when he lived in that state, so there was a chance that one of his fellow farmhands had joined up. It might be a lot to ask, but he shot a prayer heavenward that he would recognize someone when they arrived.

Dominic tried to remember what the date was. He knew

it was a Friday. Rolling his eyes upward, he calculated that it was the third of June — his mother's birthday by chance. He chose to think of that as a good omen.

It was full light when they arrived at the camp, but the men were just beginning to stir. Even though it was past five o'clock, according to Father O'Reilly, who checked his pocket watch shortly before they pulled up, they hadn't heard the bugler playing Reveille. That struck both of them as odd.

These men must have been through some wicked fighting in the last week or so, Dominic thought, *otherwise they'd be up and at 'em by now*. The horse plodded past the sentry at the perimeter of the encampment. The man merely nodded at the priest and returned to his duty of scanning the horizon.

Even though the story may have been exaggerated by the time Father Barron relayed it to him, the legend of Father O'Reilly must have had a grain of truth to it. Father Barron told him that since the beginning of the war, the priest had been aiding and ministering to thousands of wounded men, both Federal and Confederate, who had been flooding into Atlanta from battles in Tennessee and Virginia.

As the war intensified and General Sherman got closer to the gates of Atlanta, Father O'Reilly had ventured out to the camps to be of assistance to the wounded, say Mass in the field, and perform Last Rites. Apparently he was well-respected by the soldiers and officers on both sides, whether they were believers or not.

Father O'Reilly pulled the horse to a halt in the center of the camp and had Dominic disembark. He then followed suit. Rows of tents stretched out before them. Not just the wedge tents that had gained popularity as the war progressed because of their light weight and portability but even the Sibley tents. They resembled oversized teepees and could hold up to twenty men — albeit less than comfortably since they were intended to sleep only a dozen.

They needed to find the officers' headquarters. The priest walked the horse further into the camp until he spied the wall tent officers' headquarters. He tied the animal's reigns around a low-hanging branch, and then he and Dominic approached the soldier guarding the door.

After issuing Father O'Reilly a salute, the soldier inquired as to whom the priest wished to speak.

"I'd like te speak te yer commanding officer, if I may," replied the reverend.

"That would be Colonel Carter VanVleck. Let me see if he is available." The man ducked inside the tent flap. A minute later, he reemerged.

"He will see you, sir. Please step inside." He lifted the flap and allowed Father O'Reilly and Dominic to pass through.

Perusing the dimly-lit space, Dominic noticed a four-poster rope bed, a washstand equipped with a porcelain pitcher and matching basin embellished with painted wildflowers, a table covered with a starched white tablecloth, and a desk. It was his first time in an officer's tent — he was surprised to see all the luxuries housed in the nondescript enclosure.

In the center of the tent, several officers stood gathered around a large desk, looking at the map spread out before them. Seated behind the desk was the highest-ranking officer present, as Dominic determined by the silver eagle insignia on the man's shoulder strap.

When the man looked up and saw the two civilians, he stood to make introductions. "Colonel VanVleck," he said, extending his hand to the priest.

Fr. O'Reilly stepped forward and returned the handshake.

The colonel dismissed the other officers.

"It's a pleasure to meet you, Father," said Colonel VanVleck. "Your reputation precedes you, sir. I've heard tales of your care and compassion for my soldiers. Some would even say we have a saint in our midst."

"That may be a bit of an overstatement, Colonel, but I will say that God has called me te attend te the needs of all of his warring sons, and so I do the best that I can with the talents bestowed upon me."

"We thank you for that, Father. And to what do I owe the pleasure of your company today?"

"I'm here today te deliver a new recruit te ye," said the priest, indicating Dominic, who stood slightly behind him. The news may have come as a surprise, but the colonel's face didn't register anything other than the cordial look he had while meeting Father O'Reilly.

Playing his cards close to the chest — the sign of a good leader.

"Dominic Warner," he said, offering a handshake to the officer.

"Nice to meet you, Mr. Warner," the colonel replied. "We don't have civilians walking into our camp every day volunteering for service. You seem to be a young man in sound health. Up until this point in the war, what have you been doing to bide your time? I would hope you've been contributing to our cause in some respect over the last three years."

Dominic gave the report on his life just as he and Father O'Reilly had scripted. The priest nodded in agreement as the tale was unraveled. When Dominic finished, the men waited as the officer digested the information provided him.

"That seems plausible enough," he finally said. "Welcome to the United States Army, Private Warner."

He gave Dominic a salute, which he instinctively returned. *Private?* He hadn't thought of that before — of course, his corporal status would be revoked. It made him wonder how Nathan was faring. If he had somehow managed to cross lines, had he been able to retain his rank or had he been forced to start at the bottom once again as well?   If Nathan did now outrank him, Dominic was determined to have those two chevrons back in place on his sleeves as quickly as possible. Who knew, maybe he and Nathan's paths would cross again in some skirmish. He didn't want his friend to think he'd been demoted.

With Dominic taken care of, the priest excused himself to attend to the business of his flock in the camp. He assured the newly minted private that he would make his farewells before he left.

After the priest departed, Colonel VanVleck got his recruit up to speed on the most recent battle the Illinois 78th fought. From the twenty-fifth of May until the twenty-ninth, they had been entrenched at New Hope Church. Confederate General Joseph E. Johnston had retreated to Allatoona Pass several days earlier, and Major General Sherman moved around Johnston's flank rather than attack the Confederate defenses head-on. On May thirtieth, Sherman sent his troops, including the 78th Illinois, towards Dallas. They were blocked at New Hope Church by Johnston. Unfortunately, Sherman underestimated how many Confederate troops were there and he ordered General Joseph Hooker to attack. Between the rough terrain and the Confederate earthworks, they could not push Johnston's men back.

Hooker's troops suffered the brunt of the casualties. The 78th had their share as well. After both sides retreated, Colonel VanVleck gave his men some time to regroup and regain their strength. *That explained the absence of*

Reveille, Dominic surmised.

The colonel called in one of his aides and instructed him to get Dominic suited up and introduced to some of his counterparts in the camp. The man did as he was told and within half an hour the private was fitted with Union blues, including a dark blue wool coat, light blue trousers, a forage cap and, surprisingly, a pair of the ankle-high laced-up brogans. With the hot weather, he wasn't looking forward to donning the jacket, but Dominic was pleased with the bootees he was issued. None of the items were new, but the footwear was undoubtedly the nicest he'd had on his feet in ages.

It wouldn't take long for a camp follower to sew one chevron onto each of his sleeves. He'd have to find out where the ladies kept camp and look for the wife of one his fellow soldiers to do the sewing for him. He was a bit leery of the other women who tagged along after the regiments. Their function was to provide goods, such as liquor, to the men, and to provide services the military didn't supply — everything from cooking, laundering and nurse duties to things not spoken about in good company.

From his conversation with the colonel, Dominic figured it could be a few days before the next march. That down time would give him the opportunity to acclimate to his new surroundings. With his assigned gear in hand, he followed the sergeant through the camp as the man poked around each tent. Dominic thought he was looking for a particular person under whose wing he could be put. But, as it turned out, he wasn't searching, he was counting. The officer was seeking a shelter that wasn't filled to capacity.

Finally spying what he needed, he stopped in front of two men sitting in front of a fire. He introduced Dominic, then left the trio to their own devices.

"You from Illinois?" asked the younger of the two men.

"Yes, sir, I am," replied Dominic.

"No need to call me sir. I ain't got any stripes either," the man replied.

"Private Warner, can you tell me how a man manages to make it this long without Uncle Sam getting his hooks into him?" asked the older, heavier-set man. "We've been busting our tails, crisscrossing this God-forsaken land for more than two years now."

A group of men gathered around them, as this would undoubtedly be the most exciting thing to transpire in the camp the entire day.

"Didn't think I'd have to get involved," said Dominic in his best Illinois intonation. "Me and my buddy bought land in Texas back in '59, thought we'd ride out the war there, but the Reb Army had something to say about that. Earlier this year they were sending troops out to conscript any stragglers who hadn't joined their cause. Seeing the writing on the wall, me and Nathan hightailed it toward Atlanta with the thought of meeting up with Sherman's troops."

"Don't see no other newbie around. Where's your bud?" inquired the first man.

He wasn't sure if it was a lie or not, but Dominic said with a tone of regret in his voice, "Didn't make it."

The private seemed convinced but the older man looked like he had his doubts. By the murmuring Dominic heard around him, it seemed the younger man was in the minority. The other men started to verbalize their disbelief of his tale. There was a sense of hostility building.

This would be a good time for some past acquaintance to show up, thought Dominic. A moment later, he regretted that thought when he heard two familiar voices that were more than familiar to him. He immediately snapped his head around.

"Well, looky what we got here," said the first man.

"If it ain't the foul-mouth Kraut that used to work our pa's land," said the second man in an eerily similar tone.

No wonder it was said that a person should be careful what they wished for. It was none other than Billy and Danny, Hank's boys, or perhaps better known to Dominic, the spawn of Satan. *God help me.*

Chapter XXIII

The look on Jeremiah's face did not change one iota when Brigid told him her plan. He didn't register surprise, fear or disobedience. As per usual, he nodded his head, said, "Yes, Miz Brigid," and set about to do her bidding.

A person would think this was an everyday task, the way he responded, Brigid thought. She could never read that man and was somewhat uncomfortable around him because those dark brown eyes seemed to be able to look right through her. If the man had any children, she would feel sorry for them. They wouldn't be able to get away with anything.

Whatever he was thinking was none of her concern though because they needed to start preparations immediately. Brigid hurried back into the house and didn't even bother summoning her handmaid to help her pack. What was loaded on her trunks was irrelevant — she just needed to empty enough items out of her armoire so it looked like there was enough to fill all of them.

As soon as the chests were adequately full, she sent for Jeremiah and the stable boy to come and retrieve them. After they were deposited in the barn, Jeremiah's job was to empty them out, drill discreet air holes into the sides and then dump the articles back in. Later that night when it was completely dark and the house settled down, Brigid would fetch the runaways from the root cellar, and they would seclude themselves in the barn until it was time to load the coach the next morning.

She felt guilty about it, but earlier that day, Brigid absconded a flask of whiskey from the side cabinet in her father's study. It was uncharacteristic of her to take something that wasn't hers, but she vowed to bring it back when she could. There really wasn't much choice. She needed a sedative for the babies to assure they stayed quiet in the morning when they were loaded into the trunks with their mothers. Undoubtedly, everyone in Brigid's family would be up early to make their goodbyes to her as she prepared to leave Dallas. If either child made a peep, everything would be ruined, and the repercussions could very well cost someone their life.

The McGinnis family spent the afternoon together. Her father wanted to take his wife and children on an outing to visit some of their friends and neighbors to let them know Brigid was leaving to join the convent. She had mixed feelings as she received their well wishes from everyone because she still wasn't completely sure this would ultimately be her life's path. But there was no use worrying about it, as, for the time being, this was the prescribed plan and she could do nothing to change it.

It was a pleasant day. With her father at home, her mother always seemed more like the attentive parent Brigid remembered. The little girls were in seventh heaven, getting to spend a block of time with their father, who was normally working or traveling.

They had a lunch packed for them by Beulah. When the group arrived at the grassy spot where they intended to picnic, Jeremiah fetched a tablecloth to spread on the ground and the place settings. To Brigid's surprise, her mother instructed him on the exact placement of each plate, cup and bowl. She was bossing him around, albeit in a gentle way, just as she did with all the household help before the sadness had engulfed her.

Seeing her mother come to life before her gave Brigid hope. When Mrs. McGinnis directed Jeremiah to turn each plate so that the flower pattern was facing exactly the same direction, Brigid sensed her mother had reached a turning point. It would be easier to leave the house with renewed hope that her mother may be on the verge of taking back her former duties overseeing the operation of the household. *Hopefully, this isn't just wishful thinking.*

After lunch, Agnes and Martha got to take their shoes off and dip their feet in the pond nearby. Brigid's job was to keep an eye on them, which she did, but she was also able to take a few sideways glances at her parents now and then. The two sat side by side and seemed to enjoy each other's company. Witnessing the tranquil scene, Brigid thought back to the slip of paper she found the night before. As he sat shoulder to shoulder with his wife, her father looked so caring. It made Brigid wonder if the candlelight had caused her to misinterpret what she saw written on the bill of sale.

She had seen plantation owners and how they treated their slaves. It was impossible for her to imagine her father behaving in such a fashion. Perhaps it had all been a mistake. For now, she just wanted to drink in the picture before her and remember the joy and the laughter she heard in her sisters' voices and the concern she saw her father show her mother. Tomorrow would come soon enough.

The day did come fast. After staying up until after midnight to get the fugitives settled in the barn, she had precious few hours of sleep. If the rooster hadn't been crowing directly below her window when the sun peeked over the horizon, she probably would have overslept.

After stretching, she got up, slipped into the clothes she'd laid out the night before and then packed the few items remaining on her nightstand into a valise. Walking down the hallway to the stairs, she could hear everyone else starting to get up too. Once she reached the first floor, she set the bag down and went into the dining room. Steaming food was sitting in bowls, waiting to be dished up.

Since it would be her last day at their house for the foreseeable future, she had directed the cook to prepare her favorite items for the breakfast menu. The spread that morning included biscuits and gravy, scrambled eggs and bacon. She was surprised to see Beulah pouring a cup of coffee into the bone china cup next to her place at the table. *It is nice to finally be acknowledged as an adult, even if only by a servant.*

The rest of the family soon joined her and as early as it was, the little girls were chatting away like magpies. Her mother was enjoying her coffee and her father was reading the paper and getting worked up about something or other in the news. It was a scenario reminiscent of many a morning in their house before the war started.

When everyone finished eating, they filed out the back door and walked to the coach. It was loaded up and ready to go. Brigid felt a sense of reassurance seeing the three trunks lined up side by side in the back of the vehicle.

Her father was less than assured by the sight before him.

"Why in God's name are you bringing three trunks with you to the convent, young lady?" he demanded. "You know you're taking a vow of poverty, do you not?"

"Of course, Father," said Brigid. "Those trunks are filled with all my worldly goods. I intend to offer them to the sisters when I get there — they can donate them to the poor."

"And what exactly will the underprivileged do with ball gowns, may I ask?"

"The same thing I did," said Brigid in a light tone. "Wear them. Besides, they aren't all gowns. There are day frocks and other practical things like shoes and capes and undergarments." Brigid added that last tidbit to assure that her father wouldn't start digging through her trunks. Lying wasn't her forte, but she must have done reasonably well because it looked like he seemed to buy the story.

Her father shook his head. "Women," he muttered. "Brigid, if, God forbid, you do not profess your final vows, I am not replacing the items you've donated. You may want to think twice before you give everything away."

"I am comfortable with my decision, sir," she said resolutely.

"Good, because there is no changing your mind at this point," he responded.

A sense of relief washed over her — she had cleared that hurdle. Jeremiah was waiting to hand her up onto the wooden seat, so Brigid turned to each of her sisters, gave them a hug, and reminded them to be good little girls and obey their mother and father. When she approached her mother, the woman put her right hand up to her daughter's cheek.

Brigid nearly recoiled — it had been so long since her mother touched her in any manner, the motion startled her.

"I pray you've found the ideal situation, dear, and that the life of a religious suits you." She stroked her cheek. "If things don't work out, know you'll always be welcome here."

Brigid remained still, embracing the words her mother spoke to her. Tears formed in the corner of her eyes. Her father interrupted the tender interaction.

"Mrs. McGinnis, don't plant ideas in her head. We've thought this whole thing through from every angle. Of course, it will work out as it should," he said, not realizing he was contradicting his earlier statement.

He tugged Brigid's elbow to turn her in his direction. "I expect you to attend to your studies and follow the example set by the good women who have been charged with your training. The Lord will show you that you've made the proper choice."

"Yes, Father," said Brigid.

"Godspeed on your journey, daughter."

"Thank you, sir."

"Off you go," he said, whisking her in the direction of the coach.

"Jeremiah, get her there safely. I'll expect to see you back here by mid-afternoon."

"Yes, master," said the man.

Brigid listened to the exchange, and even though she had heard Jeremiah refer to her father as master before, she hadn't given it any thought until now. *Was that evidence that he was, in fact, a slave?* There was no way on earth she would broach the topic with him, but it did make her wonder.

Her father folded his arms across his chest — the stance he typically held when watching his orders being executed. Jeremiah assisted Brigid up the step. He then went to the other side and settled himself on the seat. A crack of the whip set the horses in motion. As they started down the driveway, Brigid turned and waved goodbye to her family. She had no idea how long it would be before she would be with them again.

Throughout the trip, Brigid was lost in thought, considering what may lay before her. Thankfully, the journey was uneventful. Brigid was glad they were heading away from the battlefront. It would be nice to leave the sound of gunfire behind her. She had heard enough over four weeks to last her a lifetime. As they neared their destination, she spelled out the details to Jeremiah about what she planned to do when they arrived at the Sisters of Mercy motherhouse.

When they arrived in Cartersville, they pulled up to an austere brick building. A woman in full habit stepped out to greet them. Jeremiah helped Brigid down from the vehicle. The sister approached Brigid and asked if she was the new recruit they were awaiting. When she assured her she was, the bespectacled stick-thin woman then introduced herself as Mother Mary Catherine, foundress of the Sisters of Mercy convent in Chattanooga.

"If you have everything," said the sister as she looked at the satchel Brigid held in her left hand, "then you can dismiss your driver and we'll go meet the other members of the order."

"That sounds lovely, Mother Mary Catherine, but this isn't everything. Would you happen to have someone to assist Jeremiah in unloading the rest of my items? A strong male would be preferable." The woman looked at Brigid quizzically and then glanced past her shoulder to the vehicle. Her eyes widened as she counted the trunks.

"You do know we have a vow of poverty here, right?"

"That's exactly what my father asked me," said Brigid, brightly. "I will assure you, just as I did my father, I am quite aware of that."

"Then explain the excess luggage, if you will."

"I will be happy to do that once everything is inside," said Brigid.

The sister raised an eyebrow. It was obvious the woman was used to utter compliance. Brigid hoped she wasn't starting off on a bad foot with her.

"Poverty, chastity, obedience. You would do well to remember those three words," uttered the sister. Her conscience bothered her a bit, but the ends would justify the means.

Regardless of what the mother superior thought, she

didn't deny the request. Instead, she turned and walked back into the convent. Another sister stood just inside the doorway. Mother Mary Catherine said something to her and the woman scurried off. Within a minute, an elderly man with fair skin and thin white hair came hobbling out of the building. He walked to the rear of the wagon. After Jeremiah shifted the first trunk to the back edge, the two men hoisted it up and the black man, who looked to be carrying the bulk of the weight, backed into the building, with the older man struggling to keep up.

The same routine was followed twice more. Brigid worried about the old man, whose face turned brighter red with each load. He probably had twenty years on Jeremiah. She was more than relieved when the last trunk was safely stowed in the hallway.

After peeking her head inside the entryway, she was assured everything was set in place. Brigid thanked Jeremiah for his assistance and sent him on his way.

Once inside the building, she asked the mother superior if they could be alone for a moment. The sister nodded towards her assistant, who took her leave from them.

"This is highly unusual, Miss McGinnis. What exactly is going on here?"

"Unusual may be an understatement, Mother." Brigid went to the first trunk, opened it, and moved aside a piece of clothing. Alice's brother unfolded himself from inside the box. He stood up, stepped out of the enclosure, stretched a bit and went to the next trunk. He opened it while Brigid approached the third trunk.

The sister, who Brigid guessed was normally unflappable, emitted a gasp when she saw the first scene. The second and third trunks were opened and two Negro women, each with a baby in their arms, peeked up over the top of the trunk, slowly stood up and stepped out. The woman then walked to the windows and shut the curtains.

She then turned to Brigid.

"What in the name of the good Lord have you brought here?" she demanded to know. "Have you come to our order under duplicitous terms?"

"No, Mother Mary Catherine." Brigid stood tall, certain she had done the right thing, but she trembled a bit, nervous about the woman's reaction. "My intentions are completely honorable, let me assure you. These people, who stand before you, need safe passage out of Georgia. I had them accompany me with the hope that they could find refuge here for a few days. One of the children is suffering from an ailment of the lungs. It may be serious."

"Are you telling me these people are runaway slaves?" asked the nun, lowering her voice. The man and two women in question stood quietly looking at them.

"They are," admitted Brigid. "But, if you were to hear their story, I know you would feel a sense of compassion for the plight they've endured, just as I have."

"No need to waste your breath, Miss McGinnis. I know exactly how to deal with them."

Chapter XXIV

"'Bout time you showed up, Kraut," said Billy. "We was wonderin' where you been hidin' all this time."

"You heard my story, Billy. Rest assured, I wasn't concealing myself to avoid service to our country." Dominic dropped the feigned accent he used addressing the other men. "I've been working my own land all these years, which, I would imagine, is more than you and Danny can say for yourselves."

"My, oh my, he's a fancy talker now, ain't he, Danny?" said the man to his brother. "Looks like ya got all high and mighty on us since we last saw yer sorry hide."

"Well, we know he's an Illinois man," said one of the bystanders, after listening to their exchange. "Ain't nothing to see here." The crowd dispersed. Dominic figured the men were somewhat disappointed. They were probably hoping to rat out a spy or, at the least, see a good fistfight — anything to relieve the monotony that took over camp when they were between campaigns.

The three men didn't have time to engage in any further conversation because they were called to attention by the commanding officer, who, to no one's surprise, was gathering the men to drill. That worked out well for Dominic. He wasn't all that interested in conversing with those two dimwits anyhow. He was looking forward to getting in front of his superiors to show off his skills so he could jockey for that promotion.

For an hour the troops marched back and forth in every combination of which the officer could conceive. Dominic was convinced there'd be no promotion coming from that exercise, regardless of how straight a line he could walk or how precise of a ninety-degree corner he could maneuver. The real test would come if he had the chance to show off his marksmanship skills.

Luck was on his side — later that afternoon they had a chance to do just that and, to make it even sweeter, Dominic avoided being paired with either of his two old antagonists. Good thing, or he may have been tempted to do a little target practice on them.

It was obvious that the Union troops had an abundance of ammunition because they were allowed to shoot from numerous distances using a copious amount of shot. That would never have been permissible in a Reb camp. They counted every last piece of lead. If the soldiers were allowed target practice, they would be tasked with digging out the shot afterwards from the piece of wood they targeted, since every bit was needed in the field of battle.

Just as he figured, Dominic was able to outshoot his compatriots at any distance. As fortune would have it, it was under the watchful eye of the sergeant overseeing the range.

"You," he said, pointing to Dominic. "Get over here."

"Yes, sir," he replied, hustling to where the man stood, anxious to hear the words of praise he knew he had coming.

"Where'd you learn to shoot like that, son?"

"On the open range, sir."

"Is that so? A lot of the fellows here come from farms and ranches, but no one can match your skills."

Dominic nodded, doing his best to look humble.

"You sure you didn't have some other training along the way? Maybe some military instruction you're forgetting to mention to me?"

"No, sir," said Dominic after swallowing a lump in his throat. "Guess the good Lord just blessed me in this area."

"Did the big fellow bless you with any other military skills — maybe hand-to-hand combat?"

"That would be hard to say, sir, since I haven't had the opportunity to try that," replied Dominic. No matter how he polished this one up, it was a full-out lie.

"Well then, son, it's your lucky day," said the sergeant.

Lucky? That was questionable. He could just imagine what the man was conjuring up.

"Let's have a little sparring contest, shall we? We'll find someone to take you on."

How about let's not, thought Dominic, but he didn't dare say it out loud. This could really put him in a fix. His sparring skills outpaced his shooting proficiency — Nathan would vouch for that. But if he fought all out, the sergeant would have a hard time believing he garnered those abilities on a ranch. On the other hand, if he didn't give it his all, chances were he'd get his rear end handed to him on a platter. The last thing he wanted was to be banged up before they even started their march.

The sergeant wasted no time finding a match for him. A private, about his height, but of a slighter build, was chosen from the crowd that was beginning to gather around them. There would be no weapons, just good old-fashioned grappling.

Dominic did his best to make it look like the private was putting up a good fight, but he could have slapped him away as easily as a mosquito. Figuring most people would have given him the advantage because of his more muscular build, Dominic decided to end the bout after thirty seconds and threw the young man to the ground.

The fellow's buddies picked him up and dragged him to the edge of the field.

Seeing that it may not have been a fair fight, the sergeant dismissed the private and then scanned the crowd. Dominic's eyes followed his.

Anyone but him, he thought as he spied Billy in the mix with his sidekick Danny close by as usual.

Sure enough, that was the person to whom the sergeant pointed.

Okay, I lied, but you know I'll be confessing it the next time I'm in church, thought Dominic, glancing upward. *And I promise I won't wait another ten years to get in the confessional.*

Apparently, The All Knowing One wasn't open to bargaining, because Dominic saw that thorn in his side from his childhood, who was a good half a head taller than him, approaching. The grin on his face and his arrogant stride showed he was anticipating the match.

Help me, Saint Joseph. That was the last thought he had time for before Billy came barreling at him. Using the speed he had picked up wrestling with Nathan, Dominic slipped out of the way and the bigger man tumbled past him.

Incensed, Billy scrambled up, and went to swipe his arm around Dominic's neck. Seeing his intention, Dominic ducked and hoisted himself straight at Billy's stomach, picking the man completely off his feet. He unceremoniously dropped him to his back, knocking the wind out of him. Gasping for breath, Billy looked up at Dominic and said, "Ya better run now, because when I get up, I'm goin' ta kill ya, Kraut."

The sergeant, realizing Billy wouldn't actually be rising anytime soon, turned to Dominic, pointed at his chest and said, "My quarters, now."

Dominic brushed himself off and immediately strode after the man. He hadn't walked more than ten steps when he heard the buglers tapping out the call to arms. The sergeant pivoted towards him. "We'll resume this conversation when we come back. Get your weapon and gather with the rest of the men."

"Yes, sir." Dominic saluted his commanding officer.

The camp was in an uproar, as everyone raced to the tents to gather their gear. Everything was hastily packed and once the men were loaded up and assembled, the march began. They were heading north — word circulated among the troops that their destination was Marietta, which was twenty miles away. It would take them a good portion of the day to get the men, wagons and mounted guns there.

Most of the soldiers, Dominic included, were in no mood to talk as they trudged forward. They were headed off to another battle and, inevitably, some of them wouldn't be returning. It was the nature of the game.

As Dominic filed along, keeping the spacing even between himself and the soldier in front of him, he thought back as far as he could remember, contemplating the life he had lived up to this point. It made him think of Ecclesiastes 3:1-10. For the life of him, he couldn't remember the verse word for word but felt he needed to review it. Reaching up with his free left hand, he pulled the Bible out of the inside pocket of his overcoat. He was able to page through the book while keeping cadence with the other men.

Finding the chapter, he began to read to himself. "*There is a season for everything, a time for every occupation under heaven: A time for giving birth, a time*

*for dying; a time for planting, a time for uprooting what
has been planted. A time for killing, a time for healing; a
time for knocking down, a time for building. A time for
tears, a time for laughter, a time for mourning, a time for
dancing. A time for throwing stones away, a time for
gathering them, a time for embracing, a time to refrain
from embracing. A time for searching, a time for losing;
a time for keeping, a time for discarding. A time for
tearing, a time for sewing, a time for keeping silent, a
time for speaking. A time for loving, a time for hating; a
time for war, a time for peace. What do people gain from
the efforts they make? I contemplate the task that God
gives humanity to labor at."*

The verse was eerily apropos. Thinking through the
various lines, some stood out for him. The time for
planting was when he and Nathan began their ranching
career. A time for birth — watching the animals bring forth
newborns each spring. The time for knocking down had
been just hours ago, wrestling Billy. A time for mourning
— losing his parents and, though he'd never say it out loud,
walking away from that remarkable woman he left behind
just days ago. A time for laughter made him think of the
light moments he shared with Brigid over their evenings
together. A time for embracing — he fondly recalled the
special night he got to hold that beauty in his arms as she
slept.

A time for keeping silent — he was in the midst of that
as he hid his past. A time for war, that seemed never-
ending. He prayed the time of peace would not be too far
away. But at this very moment, he fervently offered
prayers to Saint Joseph that he would survive this
skirmish. Then, for good measure, he added a prayer to his
patron saint, Saint Dominic, who was the patron of those
falsely accused. If he did survive this encounter with the

Confederate Army, he prayed he would be able to clear himself with the sergeant and avoid a potential court-martial.

Prayers were answered that day, as they always were — in the manner God determined. Those skills Dominic had been blessed with by his maker, and honed with the Rebel Army, came into play as his shots rang true. When his ammunition ran out, he was able to dispose of more men in hand-to-hand combat. While the encounter felt like it lasted hours, it was probably forty-five minutes all told. But a lot of damage can happen in a short time. Both sides had numerous casualties and pulled back to regroup for their next encounter.

Dominic had seen his share of dead men in his life — it was the reality of war. But when he walked past the spot where the orderlies were lining up the newly deceased, his eye caught one body and his feet refused to step any further. The man's midsection was splattered in blood, but his visage was unblemished — it was the sergeant he had the run-in with earlier in the day. A feeling of guilt engulfed him. He had prayed he would be able to get out from under the scrutiny of his superior, but he never meant to clear his name by the man's death. Dominic felt horrible, but realized, if the man found his way to heaven, he would surely know the younger soldier's intentions were honorable.

For all he knew, the man may not care at all — if he had lived his life according to the Church, he could at this very moment be traipsing the streets of gold; wandering around and shooting the breeze with other friends who had gone before him. For that man and all the other fallen soldiers, their earthly cares had been set aside. *Perhaps in heaven a person's perspective changes*, Dominic mused. He prayed the dead forgave all the wrongs done to them whilst they had dwelt among their fellow mortals. *Forgive us our trespasses as we forgive those who trespass against us.*

Chapter XXV

The only noise in the hallway was the sound of two cooing babies. Brigid and the three others stood motionless as they waited to hear the mother superior expound on her remarks.

The lady in question looked at the four of them, then making the Sign of the Cross, called for Sister Mary Peter. When the younger sister walked into the area, she was introduced as Mother Mary Catherine's assistant.

"Sister Mary Peter, as you can see, we have guests. This young lady is…" she paused, pointed to one of the women, and looked at Brigid for an answer.

"That's Alice, Mother Superior, and the infant is her son Josiah."

"Nice to meet you, Alice," said the mother superior, with a nod.

"And you, as well, ma'am," replied Alice.

"Whom do we have here?" she asked, looking at the man who stood between the two women, acting as their protector.

"My name is Marcus. Miz Alice's brother. And this be my woman Daisy and our son Abraham."

"Abraham, say you? That's a fine name. Let's pray he will grow up to be as honorable a man as our president, Mr. Abraham Lincoln."

"That's the fellow he's named for," said Marcus.

Brigid could hardly believe her ears. It was hard to decide what was more shocking — that there were sisters in

Georgia who were Unionists or that slaves were abreast of current political events.

"Mr. Marcus, you said Daisy is your woman. Is she not your wife?"

"No, ma'am," said the man with a note of shame in his voice. "Our master never gave us permission to jump the broom."

"That can be remedied easily enough. We've a priest close by and plenty of sisters to act as witnesses. It won't do for Abraham's paternity to be in question."

Daisy's face lit up. "Thank you, ma'am," she said shyly.

"It's my pleasure — and I presume the Lord will delight in seeing you legally wed as well."

She turned to Sister Mary Peter. "Get a couple of rooms aired out for our guests. They'll be with us until the baby is ready to travel again. Send a message to the station master at the next stop that we have passengers who will be ready for pick-up in a week or two."

"Yes, Mother Superior."

"Alice, Sister Mary Peter will take charge of your group while you are on our premises. You have my word that she can be trusted. After all, she took her name in honor of our Blessed Mother, who along with her husband, Saint Joseph, and son, Jesus, was a fugitive herself. Saint Peter is the patron saint of slaves. You'll be in good hands with her."

Dropping to her knees, Alice made the Sign of the Cross, and started praying.

"*Ave Maria, gratia plena, Dominus tecum. Benedicta tu in mulieribus, et benedictus fructus ventris tui, Iesus. Sancta Maria, Mater Dei, ora pro nobis peccatoribus, nunc, et in hora mortis nostrae. Amen.*"

The woman was praying the Hail Mary in Latin. Brigid

looked at her as if she'd grown two heads. *Negroes are Catholic?* It certainly appeared this one was. She had never even considered such a thing before. Witnessing that made Brigid question much of what her father had told her through the years. The man had purposely misled her. *But why would he do such a thing?*

The mother superior instructed the fugitives to follow the younger sister, who would show them where to freshen up. They were told they could look through a closet for clothes to replace the ones they wore, with the expectation they could pass as free blacks once they left the convent.

The three adults each thanked the older sister and then followed behind Sister Mary Peter as she headed towards the living quarters of the convent.

When the group left the room, Mother Mary Catherine turned her attention to Brigid.

"Thank you, young lady, for bringing this precious cargo safely to us."

"You're welcome, Mother Superior," she stammered out.

"Are you an experienced conductor or is this your maiden voyage, my dear?"

Brigid looked at the nun in confusion.

"I beg your pardon?"

The sister narrowed her eyes and looked closer at Brigid. "How did you come upon these people that you brought here today?"

"I found Alice and her baby in the barn on our property one night. She led me to her brother and his family, who were hiding in our root cellar. Alice implored me not to turn them over to the authorities. Her master is the father of her baby, and he wanted her to dispose of it before it was born. She couldn't bring herself to punish the child for the sins of its father."

"I see," said Mother Mary Catherine. "Tell me why you brought them here with you."

"Of course, Mother," said Brigid. "I imagine you were aware that I would be joining the Sisters of Mercy before I even knew. By chance, my father arrived home from Virginia the same night I encountered Alice. He informed me that he had chosen an order for me and I would be leaving our house less than a day later to take my place here. It was all in God's timing, as they say, because it proved to be the ideal moment to get them off our property. I took our driver Jeremiah into my confidences, and he helped me transport these people to your door."

"Do you intend to make your vows with us, Miss McGinnis?" the sister asked.

Brigid looked at the toes of her kid boots peeping out from the bottom of her day dress.

"That is my father's intention and, until two weeks ago, that was my intention as well. Now, I'm not so sure." Her cheeks started to burn. "Something happened that has caused me to have other considerations."

"Would that be something or someone?" Mother Mary Catherine asked. She raised her eyebrows. Brigid had a feeling the woman may have heard such a tale before.

That was a topic Brigid would rather not discuss with anyone — unless it was brought up in the confessional. She skirted around it.

"There is a time of discernment here, is there not?"

"Of course, my dear. You may spend up to twelve months as a postulant. If, after that time, you decide to continue the process, you will be admitted as a novitiate."

Brigid was tempted to let out a sigh of relief, but she caught herself.

"Back to the cargo you brought to our door, are you aware of any other runaways using your root cellar for shelter?"

"I can't say for sure, but it seems that whenever my father travels, I hear unexplained noises coming from below the house. It could be because of the placement of my bedroom, but I seem to be the only one in my family who has heard anything."

Again Brigid had to question; were the servants involved in this business? The more she thought about it, the more she wondered if their house was part of the network of stops on the Underground Railroad. Had this subterfuge been going ever since her father took his position in Virginia? If so, how many people had stayed on their property before she stumbled upon Alice and her family?

The sister interrupted Brigid's reverie.

"I suspect what you may be thinking. So I will confirm your suspicions. Yes, your residence is a known safe spot for our travelers."

Brigid wasn't sure how to take the news. Slavery was woven into the fabric of life in the South. People even used Biblical principles to justify it. Just as Jesus had said, "The poor you will always have," she had been taught that slavery would always be a part of human history.

Now, she didn't know what to think. The Sisters of Mercy obviously did not support it and, as a matter of fact, they were doing what they could to help their fellow human beings out of bondage. There was a war being waged to determine if slavery would be allowed in the United States any longer. If the Confederate States lost the war, which at this point looked more likely to happen than not, then slavery would be outlawed in the whole country.

Should I just let everything play out, or should I take a

stand for these people now? It wasn't like Brigid to go against the majority opinion, and it most certainly wasn't like her to break any laws, but something needed to be done.

"Sister, what can I do to help them?"

"I knew you'd come around," she replied. "With the name Brigid, it is your destiny to assist God's broken children."

"I'm not sure I understand what you mean, Mother Superior."

"Were you not aware that your namesake, Saint Brigid of Kildare, is the patron saint of fugitives?"

The thought brought goose pimples to Brigid's arms. She hadn't known that. "Mother Superior, tell me what you'd like me to do."

"I want you to think this through before you agree, but if you are willing, we could use your help picking up another load of passengers from your house."

Brigid's mouth went dry. It was one thing supporting a cause verbally, but actually putting her life on the line to help was a completely different story. But, now that she was aware of how wretched life was for the slaves, how could she turn a blind eye to the situation?

"No need to answer now, my dear. Let God speak to your heart. We'll cross that bridge when we come to it. For the time being, let's get you started on your studies. That is why you're here, after all."

"Yes, Mother Superior."

"Sister Mary Peter will show you to your room when she gets back. Get settled in, then come and share a meal with your fellow sisters. You'll want a good night's rest — our days start early here."

By early, the sister meant before the sun even thought of

peeking over the eastern horizon. The next morning, Brigid was awakened by a soft tapping on the door of the austere room in which she slept. She rubbed her eyes, trying to gather her bearings and recall where she was. In a moment, it came to her, and she sat up in the narrow cot and reached for the flint to light the candle on her nightstand. She didn't want to be late for Lauds on her first day, so she'd have to quickly make her bed and get dressed on her own — she didn't have Tilly to assist her anymore.

With the light from the candle filling the corners of the room, she spied a tunic hanging from the hook on the far wall. She would wear the simple gray habit with a plain gray veil until she made her first vows.

Life for the Sisters of Mercy revolved around routine, mainly prayer. After Lauds, breakfast was served by the women assigned to cooking detail. Then it was back to the chapel for Morning Prayer, which was followed by Mass. Next, the postulants went to theology class, which was taught by their pastor. At noon, Midday Prayer was sung. Singing was required of all the women in the community. Brigid found it uncomfortable because she distinctly recalled her mother's reaction to her warbling. But, to her surprise, several of the other postulants complimented her on her voice. It would be a sin to lie, so Brigid was sure their praise was genuine. When she thought about it, she considered that perhaps it wasn't her voice her mother objected to; maybe it was singing in general since it brought back memories of Baby John.

After lunch, the sisters did the work they needed to accomplish for the day. The postulants went back to focus on topics including Church history, philosophy, geography, Latin, earth science and mathematics. Brigid didn't say this to anyone, but class time was her favorite part of the day — her love for learning was insatiable.

Contemplative prayer and prayerful reading, namely perusing passages from the Bible, was next on the afternoon agenda. Vespers, sung in Latin, began at five o'clock, and, afterward, the women made their way to the dining area for supper. After the meal, the Rosary was recited and, at eight o'clock, Night Prayer commenced. The evening concluded in complete silence, which was to be maintained until Lauds the next morning.

Chapter XXVI

The event surrounding the loss of the sergeant's life didn't stop Dominic from praying, but he was much more judicious when he offered up his entreaties to the litany of saints. There was no time to dwell on it, anyhow. Every few days, his regiment would take up arms again and return to the field in what came to be known as the Battle of Marietta.

General Johnston was entrenched outside Marietta — halfway between Atlanta and the northern border of Georgia. Major General Sherman engaged his counterpart over the course of four weeks in a series of battles, which started on the fourteenth of June at Pine Mountain.

The most famous casualty that day was Confederate General Leonidas Polk, second cousin of the late U.S. President James Polk. He was killed by a shell while scouting enemy positions with General Johnston, General William J. Hardee and their staffs. Their observation outpost was abandoned the next day.

That same day, the Illinois 78th was back at it again, this time at Gilgal Church. Word had it they'd be facing Reb troops under the guidance of Major General Patrick Cleburne. A native of Ireland, the man was legendary for having scaled the ranks of the Confederate Army from private to major general in the span of one year's time. The most controversial decision he was known for was proposing to President Davis, in January of 1864, that slaves should be armed — with the thought that in time they could earn their freedom. The proposal was not received well by Davis and company and thus never enacted.

While that declaration was contentious, Dominic and his regiment witnessed another command from Cleburne that made them wonder about his state of mind. When their commander advanced on the major general and his troops, he ordered his men to reinforce the main line with wood taken from the church. The Union Army watched Gilgal Church being dismantled by the Rebel soldiers while they were under artillery and light arms fire.

By the time the church was completely disassembled, the firing was coming at them in full force. The engagement lasted less than an hour, but, in the end, Cleburne's position was untenable and he was ordered to withdraw.

Dominic and his fellow infantrymen may not have been upper brass, but they were smart enough to see the folly of disrespecting a house of worship. Getting the Almighty One riled up was never a good idea.

On the eighteenth of June, they were given a reprieve as Johnston partially withdrew to protect his supply lines. It was a blessing for both sides as they were in the second straight week of rain and the conditions, trying to hold their ground, were nothing short of treacherous.

The next encounter for the Illinois 78th was on the twenty-second of June at Kolb's Farm. Lt. General John B. Hood attempted to attack the Union forces, but poor terrain led to the failure of that mission.

It struck Dominic that any piece of land could become a battleground — *didn't matter if it was a town, city, mountain, building or something as obscure as some poor farmer's yard*. Wherever the opposing forces met head to head, they fought it out. He prayed his ranch would be spared and the war would peter out before it reached that far west.

The last action they saw in June started on the twenty-seventh at Kennesaw Mountain. It was the most significant frontal assault Sherman had ever launched against Johnston's Confederate Army of Tennessee. The endeavor turned out to be unsuccessful and costly and resulted in high casualties for the Union Army. However, good fortune, or the Lord's grace, continued to be on Dominic's side as he made it through another major encounter none the worse for the wear.

While Kennesaw Mountain was considered a tactical defeat for the Union forces, it failed to deliver what the Confederacy needed the most — a halt to Sherman's advance on Atlanta. Consequently, Johnston was relieved of his command of the Confederate Army.

In the end, the Union Army declared Kennesaw Mountain a victory. The 1864 Fourth of July celebration for the Union Army, 2nd Brigade, 2nd Division, XIV Corps, 78th Illinois Volunteer Infantry Regiment, or what remained of it, was one for the books. The same could be said for most of the regiments under Sherman's command at that time. There was no doubt now that the odds of the Union Army winning the war were significantly in their favor.

Chapter XXVII

It was not often that anything interrupted the routine the Sisters of Mercy had maintained for decades. That was why Brigid was startled one evening to hear someone knocking at the entrance to the convent. She scurried to the door so the noise didn't wake the babies. With the little one finally on the mend and the next depot spot prepared for them, they were set to make their departure in the next twenty-four hours. Brigid pulled the door open. Looking at the person standing directly before her, her knees buckled and her hands began to shake. *What in the name of heaven would bring Stewart Williams to the door of any convent, let alone this one?*

Her first instinct was to slam the door, but she could not command her arm to do her bidding, so she stood there staring at him like a dolt. For some reason, he stared back as if he were just as surprised to see her as she was to see him.

Stewart was able to gather his wits about him quicker than she and spoke first.

"So, if it isn't Miss Brigid, or should I say, Sister Brigid. Didn't I just see you walking around in layman's clothes this spring? Who'd have thought I'd run across you in little ol' Cartersville."

"The same can be said of you," replied Brigid coldly. "But it is still Miss Brigid. I've just started my studies."

Gripping tightly onto the door handle, she gathered her courage and asked him point blank, "What business do you have here?"

"That's a good question, Miss Brigid, so I'll be succinct. I've got some property that's gone missing. I was out of town on business and circumstances beyond my control delayed my return to our plantation. Upon my arrival, I was apprised of the situation. Immediately, I rounded up the bloodhounds and started tracking."

If it involved animals, Brigid had a sense of what business he had been about. She tried not to shiver thinking of it.

"The trail may have been a bit cold, but, interestingly enough, the dogs led me to your old place."

Brigid felt she was on the verge of swooning, but steadied herself to hear him out.

"Lo and behold, from there I was led to this building and, consequently, to you."

The man put his hands on his hips and stared at her.

For the first time in her life, Brigid looked Stewart straight in the eyes. That's when she noticed their unusual color. The enormity of the situation hit her head on — his eyes were identical in color to baby Josiah's.

Chapter XXVIII

Dominic caught the attention of an officer during the Marietta campaign. It wasn't for censure, as it had been with the ill-fated sergeant, but for the commendation he originally hoped he would have coming to him. Arriving back at camp one day, he felt a bit leery when he was called to the captain's quarters. The guard on duty led him into the tent and Dominic was saluted by the commanding officer. He automatically saluted back. The captain then stepped towards him and ceremoniously awarded him a set of chevrons with three bars. His meritorious service during battle earned him a promotion to sergeant in the United States Army.

At this point those extra stripes wouldn't be worth a hill of beans — the Rebs weren't counting, they were just shooting. That was abundantly clear to Dominic when he felt himself in their crosshairs earlier that day.

The men in his regiment barely had time to down a cup of coffee and take a quick cat nap before they were called out to the battleground again. *An open field doesn't allow much cover,* Dominic mused. It was a miracle they weren't all slaughtered. By chance, when they charged the Confederate line this time around, Dominic could see Billy and Danny to his left. One thing he had to say about them, they were loyal to each other to a fault. *Guess when you grow up in a house with an ill-tempered wench like their mother, you have to find someone you can depend on to get by.*

Dominic did his best to keep low and get a graycoat in his sights before taking a shot. A marksman would be a sitting duck if they shot willy-nilly — he'd run out of ammunition long before the other side ran out of men.

Unfortunately, that was the predicament into which Danny had gotten himself — having a gun and nothing to load in it. The line of soldiers was pushing behind them so there wasn't any turning around to grab more shot from camp. Billy noticed his brother's dilemma around the same time Dominic did. He immediately put himself between Danny and the line of fire.

They hadn't walked more than eight feet when Billy took a hit directly to the chest. When he dropped, Danny went right down on his knees next to him and put one hand on top of the other over his brother's chest to stem the flow of blood spurting from the cavity in his upper body. Dominic crouched down and hustled to Billy's side as well.

"Danny," said Billy, gasping for air, "I want youse to take my gun and keep charging. I'll wait here for you."

Looking at his brother in disbelief, Danny shook his head. "I ain't going nowhere without you, Billy."

"Don't give me no guff, Danny Boy. I'm still your big brother." His breathing became more labored. "Do as I tell ya or I'll kick yer sorry rear end around the square when we get back to camp."

"Okay, Billy," said Danny with tears in his eyes.

Billy's head dropped slightly to the right and he noticed Dominic.

"Kraut," he said, with a slight smile. "Just wanted to let you know, ya beat me fair and square when we was wrasslin'." He paused and started coughing. "Do me a favor and keep an eye on Danny, will ya? We're cut from the same cloth — ain't neither of us been blessed with much smarts. But Danny, he's a good kid. I was the one egging him on all that time when we was youngins."

"You've got my word," said Dominic. He took the pistol from Billy's hand, wiped the blood off of it onto his pant leg, and handed the weapon to Danny.

"Come on, Danny. We've got some Rebs to chase down."

Danny wiped his nose with his sleeve. "You stay right here, Billy. We'll come gitcha as soon as we put a few more fellars in their grave. Got it?"

"Got it," Billy whispered.

Dominic pulled Danny by the elbow to get to the far right side of the field. They used a pile of bodies for cover. Then the two of them took aim, side by side, until the call to retreat sounded. Putting the guns back in their holsters, they stepped over fallen soldiers and made their way back to Billy. The life was gone out of him — his body was already starting to stiffen. Dominic knelt by him and closed each of the dead man's eyelids.

"Eternal rest, grant unto him, O Lord," he said, mimicking the prayer he'd learned from Brigid. "And let perpetual light shine upon him. May he rest in peace. Amen."

He made the Sign of the Cross, paused for a moment, and then he and Danny each grabbed the body under one arm and dragged it back to camp.

They never talked about the incident after that, but from that point on, the two of them called a truce. It was just as well with Dominic — he didn't like having enemies, especially when they were behind him on a battlefield with a loaded gun. You never knew when a person could take a slip and accidentally fire. It had been known to happen.

After that skirmish, word went around the camp that there would be a break in action for twenty-four hours so each side could bury their dead and get the injured men off the field and to the surgeons.

When Dominic got back to his tent, a soldier, just one rank above him, informed him that Captain Alexander C.

McClurg requested to meet with him immediately. Following the directions provided, he went straight to the captain's tent. He was met by other soldiers who had been summoned as well.

As it turned out, the men were handpicked for a mission and would be leaving the camp that afternoon. Dominic was more than ready to take on more responsibility. He didn't want to have excess time on his hands to dwell on thoughts of Brigid. Pining after her would do no good — it could cause him to lose focus, and now, more than ever, he needed to be on his toes.

The operation set before them would leave little time for daydreaming. He was assigned to one of the scouting parties that would fan out from Marietta to surrounding areas looking for pockets of resistance or assembled Confederate troops.

Dominic was glad to be dismissed from the numerous rounds of drilling his fellow soldiers would be doing over the next few hours. To make it even better, he was assigned a mount that would be his as long as he was a part of the 78th Illinois. *Of course, that was probably what they told the horse's last master — doubt if it worked out too well for that Kamerad.* Nevertheless, Dominic was happy to finally have a way to get around other than his own two feet. It had been months since he felt raw horseflesh beneath him. There was nothing like the sense of freedom sitting atop a powerful steed, galloping unchecked, and letting the wind whisk away all the cares of the world.

Riding gave Dominic a feeling of connectedness with his ancestors. His father's family had raised Bavarian Warmbloods for generations. Now that his memory was fully restored, Dominic recalled life in their homeland before he and his parents immigrated to the United States. He had ridden horses since he was a toddler.

The Bavarians on his uncle's farm were huge, at least from his perspective at such a young age. They were close to sixteen hands in height and known for their energy, long strides, jumping ability and temperament. While Dominic knew it would be unrealistic to be assigned a horse with such a stellar lineage, he still looked forward to meeting his new mate — regardless of its breed.

Even during a time of war, God maintained his sense of humor, Dominic realized. When he walked to the pen on the edge of camp, the private accompanying him pointed out the horse to which he was assigned.

Not only was it nearly impossible to guess its breed, but the only way it would approach sixteen hands would be if the hands measuring it were the size of Brigid's. He doubted if the horse could carry a rider much bigger than that sprite. But what the horse lacked in size, she made up for in spirit. He found that out the hard way when he held out his hand toward her and got nipped for his effort.

"Aren't we the cheeky one?" He shook his hand to revive the blood flow. The horse reared up as though it understood his words.

Dominic chuckled to himself thinking back to his conversation with Brigid and the topic of the Royal We.

"I have no idea what your moniker was previous to our meeting, but, since I'm dealing with royalty here, you deserve a name befitting a queen. I don't imagine Queen Victoria would mind having a fine piece of horseflesh like yourself named after her, since she is known to have an affinity for riding."

He looked the horse in the eye. "Shall we call you Victoria?" The mare did not look impressed. "Too formal? How about Vicky?" Still no positive reaction. "Your Royal Majesty?" Something about that name must have suited it because the horse reared its head back in what looked to be a sign of approval.

"Your Royal Majesty? That works for me. But seeing that we're going to be on a first-name basis, let's go with Majesty. And you may call me Dominic." He dug in his pocket for a small carrot. The horse grabbed it in its teeth, chomped it down, and nuzzled Dominic's hand looking for more.

"Who knows, maybe with your stature I'll ride low enough to keep my head attached to my shoulders and get through this war alive," Dominic said, with a tone of amusement in his voice.

After all the scouting party horses were saddled, the men met together on the eastern border of the camp. Captain McClurg grouped the men into pairs and gave them their orders. Dominic was assigned to ride with Sergeant James K. Magie. The two were instructed to go to the town of Cartersville.

On any other horse, at a trotting pace, the trip would take half a day. With Majesty, it would be anybody's guess. *Hopefully, the sergeant is a patient man*, thought Dominic.

Sergeant Magie's horse had seen better days itself so the two pairs were well-matched. After introducing themselves, they set out on their route, conversing casually on the way.

There was no point divulging any more information to the man than he needed to, so Dominic gave the sergeant the same story that he had told Colonel VanVleck. He could always fill in other inconsequential details later if the man was of a mind to learn more about him.

Sergeant Magie, or James, as he insisted on being called, was quite the verbose fellow. He was a newspaper man from McDonough County in western Illinois. He became the owner of a newspaper, called the *Macomb Journal*, just before the war broke out. Earlier that year, he had come up with an idea to pass along first-hand details of the war by writing a weekly letter home, which was published in his newspaper upon its receipt. How he found a reliable way to post the letters was beyond Dominic, but, evidently, they made their way up north somehow. James proudly told him that his weekly letter was the highlight of the paper for his readers.

The man turned out to be a valuable resource for Dominic to learn of the engagements the 78th Illinois encountered before he joined up. James had a way with words and a sense of humor similar to his own, which made the time go by faster than Dominic anticipated.

Before long, the sun was close to setting. They could see Cartersville on the horizon. It looked like such a sleepy place; neither man could imagine they'd find anything untoward there so they decided to split up to make the scouting go quicker. James would go on the main roads and Dominic would traverse the side streets. It shouldn't take more than ninety minutes to pass by every structure in the area. Then they would meet up on the far side of the town and determine where to settle in for the night.

When they parted ways, Dominic turned his horse to the right and the mare plodded down the street. On the left side, just past several modest homes, stood a church. The starlight glinted off the simple stained-glass windows. That adornment led him to believe it was a Catholic house of worship. A lone buggy was parked in front of a smaller structure adjacent to the stone building. Dominic assumed it was the convent or rectory.

Squinting, he saw a good-sized man standing on the doorstep, with his hands on his hips in an aggressive stance. Instinctively, Dominic slipped off the back of his horse and led the animal behind a clump of lilac bushes. In this case, its size was a blessing because it wouldn't be visible from the street. He tied the reins to a bough and strode towards the church, keeping himself hidden as best he could by darting from tree to tree on the opposite side of the street.

Something wasn't right about what he saw before him. Getting closer, he saw the man conversing with a petite woman. The man reached one hand toward her. With a hand that large, he was able to wrap his fingers around the lady's upper arm with room to spare.

Not knowing the man's intent, he quickened his pace to get closer so he could intercede on the woman's behalf if necessary. When he was within forty feet of them, Dominic was able to see more clearly and noticed the gray tunic the female wore.

What on earth was that man doing addressing a woman religious in such a fashion? He noticed that a gray veil covered her head— the only part of her body visible was her face. But that visage was so distinguishable that Dominic's heart nearly stopped beating— it was the face of the woman he loved and never imagined he'd see again.

Chapter XXIX

"If you lay a hand on me, Stewart, so help me, I'll scream," said Brigid icily.

"You're not going to want to do that," Stewart replied, but he nonetheless dropped his hand back to his hip. "I'd like you to step outside so we can talk."

"I have nothing to discuss with you," Brigid replied, feigning the courage she was sorely lacking.

"Actually, I think you do," said Stewart, crossing his arms in front of him. "If there's one thing the sisters taught well at Locust Grove Academy, it was mathematics. I can put two and two together. Let me lay this out for you. I own a plantation that runs on slave labor. The men, women and children living on that piece of land are my legal property. Every so often, one or two of them will get it in their head that they have the right to be free and will fashion a plan to escape."

She looked straight at him. "That's your business; it has nothing to do with me," said Brigid, in what she hoped was a steady voice.

"I'm not so sure about that, Brigid. As I told you earlier, the bloodhounds tracked the scent of my escaped slaves to your father's house. I know the man has been in attendance with President Davis for the last several months. Your poor mother has gone mad since she lost her child — or since you took his life, if what I've heard is true."

"That is a lie and you know it," Brigid spat out.

"Regardless, you do run the household in your father's absence, do you not?"

Brigid refused to answer.

"I'll take that as a yes." Stewart gave her a crooked grin. "Being part of a slave patrol isn't as easy as it was back in the day. I doubt that darkies are getting any smarter, but the hearts and heads of the do-gooders are getting softer. Seems they've developed a system for assisting the fugitives in their flight. Some call it the Underground Railroad. I trust you've heard of it?"

The lack of response on Brigid's part didn't stop Stewart from his spiel.

"Apparently, some of the houses on this network are used without the owner's permission. Your father is above reproach — I would never question his loyalty, being a slave owner himself." He stopped, as if to judge her reaction. "Seeing you're such a good Catholic girl and would never break a law, I was willing to give you the benefit of the doubt when I arrived there yesterday."

So, her suspicions had been true. Her father was involved in slave trafficking. *How could I have been so blind all these years?* She maintained her silence.

"Have I caught you off guard, Brigid? You knew your papa owned the household help, did you not? We were at auction together when he purchased a handmaid for your birthday less than two years ago. I personally inspected her myself, so I knew she would be docile and cooperative — the perfect fit for a fine young lady like yourself."

It was impossible to maintain a neutral look — her jaw tensed with the revulsion she felt for him and for every ugly word he said. Brigid bit her lower lip to keep from responding.

"Now that I think of it, you probably didn't know about your father's side business. Banking is a solid trade, but not quite lucrative enough to keep his family living in the fashion they had come to enjoy over the years. Being the respectable church-goer that Mr. McGinnis is, he kept those affairs between himself and a few fellow businessmen, including my sire. Your father really didn't want to sully his reputation by announcing to the world that he was involved in such sordid dealings. So he threatened a whipping to any of the slaves in your household who let on that they were anything other than hired help. As I was building my resume back then, I was more than happy to hone my thrashing skills on anyone who got out of line."

Fire burned inside Brigid. She couldn't imagine her father inflicting something so contemptible on another human being. *Evidentially he didn't need to — he had his henchman to do his dirty work.* She shivered.

"Speaking of whipping, that brings me back to the current situation with which we're dealing. I won't sugarcoat this, Brigid. My presumption, and I would put money on this that I'm correct, is that you've somehow been coerced into siding with the bleeding-heart abolitionists. While your father has been away on business, you've opened your home to runaway slaves."

Brigid did her best to hold his look without blinking.

"If it had been anyone else's property, I doubt that I'd be chasing these animals hither and yon, but this is personal. I need to make sure we get them back so we can use them for an example to discourage other runaways. It will be quite the spectacle for their fellow slaves to see me whip those escapees within an inch of their lives. Of course, it isn't always easy judging how much a human body can take; occasionally I get a bit overzealous."

Brigid steadied herself by grabbing onto the door frame.

"Did I mention, too, that we follow the dictates of the Fugitive Act of 1850? As slave patrollers, we are allowed to use our own good judgment to levy punishment upon those citizens who interfere with the capture of slaves. It's an unfortunate task, but someone needs to do it."

She had never heard of such a thing, but the prospect frightened her to no end. The wheels were spinning in Brigid's head. She had to craft a response to him that wouldn't incriminate anyone.

"Stewart, I have no idea what you're talking about, but even if your suppositions were true, and the people you are searching for were on these premises, this property belongs to the Catholic Church —it's a sanctuary."

"I wouldn't dare broach such sacred territory," said Stewart patronizingly. "But we have developed ways to smoke animals out." He looked at the wooden structure and nodded in satisfaction.

"You wouldn't dare burn down a convent. Have you no consideration for your soul?" exclaimed Brigid. "You would be risking the lives of all the women religious here."

"That's what we refer to as collateral damage."

Stewart may have thought Brigid's mother was unbalanced, but *he* was completely unhinged. Brigid said a quick prayer to Saint Anthony, hoping he would supply an answer to the dilemma she faced. Sure enough, within seconds, her prayer was answered. But, as most things lately seemed to go, it wasn't how she had envisioned it.

"You know, Brigid, now that I think about it..." Stewart tapped his chin in consideration. He swooped the hat off his head, held it over his heart, and nodded towards her. "Endangering one's soul is a precarious proposition, so how about I just turn around, depart from this city, and leave well enough alone?"

She wasn't fooled by the conciliatory remark. Brigid waited for him to finish his piece.

"I'm a man who is willing to compromise if the situation

warrants such an action. To be honest, the lives of those slaves mean nothing to me. But I suspect, with your tenderhearted nature, they have some significance for you." He paused to let his words sink in.

"I will let them escape Scot-free and make sure you are free from incrimination on one condition — that you accompany me back to my plantation and take my hand in marriage."

Brigid's jaw dropped open. "Are you jesting?" she asked incredulously. "What in God's name would make you put forth such an offer, and why on earth would I even consider such a thing?"

"It's a business transaction, Brigid. My parents desire to see me wed, so the family name can be passed down to my offspring. You're from an upstanding family, and, seeing how you've matured through the years, I'd say you're probably the best catch in our county."

"I'm not a horse to be sold at auction and bred," Brigid shot back with indignation.

"That's an interesting analogy," said Stewart. "Actually, you do remind me of a filly in need of a powerful man to break her. Brigid, you can be headstrong and try to resist me, but the consequences won't be pretty, let me assure you. It's your choice now — you either come along with me nice and sweet-like or I set to work with my original plan. You have ten seconds to decide."

Chapter XXX

Even though Dominic was able to cross the street undetected to get closer to the church, he wasn't there soon enough to hear the conversation between the man and the woman. But he was acquainted well enough with Brigid to determine that she was in a state of turmoil.

He could hardly believe his eyes when, after a few seconds more, the conversation concluded, and Brigid crossed the threshold of the building and drew the door shut behind her. She followed the man as he retreated to the vehicle on the road.

Brigid walked to the passenger side of the carriage and the man took a step forward and offered her his hand. She ignored the gesture and pulled herself up and sat on the far right edge of the bench. The man walked around to the other side and hoisted himself up. He grabbed a whip, and then, seeming to think better of using it, made a clicking sound to urge the horses to turn the conveyance around.

Sitting ramrod straight on the seat and turning her head away from the man, Brigid looked regal — veil and all. She seemed docile enough, but something was likely brewing beneath that surface. If he had to guess, he would say she was being forced to do something against her will.

The man grinned toward her and seemed pleased with himself. *Wonder how quickly I can knock that smirk off his face?* As gratifying as that sounded, he knew he needed to proceed with caution. His first thought was to track down James so the two of them could confront the man together, but there was no time for that.

After the vehicle was headed in the proper direction, the man urged the team to turn back onto the main street. They drove out of town on the same road Dominic and James had come in on earlier that evening. They were heading towards Dallas. It made him wonder if the man was from that area — perhaps he and Brigid were acquainted. *Maybe they've known each other their whole lives.* The thought of that beautiful young lady conversing with any man but himself caused a cloud of jealousy to engulf his mind. Yet, reading what he saw before him, if the two did know each other previously, it was a less-than- harmonious relationship.

Dominic slipped back across the street to get to Majesty. He untied the reins and mounted the horse. It didn't make sense to try to sneak up behind the vehicle — if the man was armed, someone could get hurt. He had a couple of options for how to proceed. The best bet might be to loop around to the south and get ahead of the vehicle a mile or so and then wait to confront them when they were well outside the town. At this hour, he doubted anyone would be about, but he didn't want to take any chances. It was best to be well out of the range of the ears of the townsfolk should any shooting occur.

Going with that plan, Dominic rode his horse far enough east of the road that led from Cartersville so that the occupants of the vehicle wouldn't hear the sound of his horse's hooves. He then dug his heels into Majesty's sides to get her to do a full-out gallop. She may not have been the fastest horse in the paddock, but she'd be able to outrun a pair of horses pulling a heavy conveyance for at least a mile or two — that was all he needed out of her.

After what he judged to be just over a mile, Dominic slowed the horse to a trot and turned west to position himself on the road. He wanted to intercept the carriage when it came up and over the nearby crest. That would keep him and Majesty concealed until the last moment.

The timing was ideal. Not more than two minutes after

Dominic got in position, he heard the sound of horses barreling over the hill. When the driver saw the roadway blocked and with ditches on both sides of the path, he had no other option than to pull on the reigns and stop the team.

A lone Union soldier on a craggy mare was probably the last thing the man expected to see, but he kept his reaction in check. The young lady, on the other hand, was not as adept at playing poker — she gasped when she saw him. The driver spun to face Brigid just as her hand flew up and covered her mouth. Her eyes were as wide as saucers.

He looked at her suspiciously before turning back to Dominic.

"What's the matter, Sergeant? You lose track of your Uncle Sam?"

"I should say not. As a matter of fact, he and Honest Abe got me on a mission tonight. Looking for Reb stragglers. It seems to me I've found one."

"As you can see, officer, I wear no uniform. I'm just a civilian minding my own business."

"And what business would that be that involves traveling with a woman of the cloth unescorted in the middle of the night?" asked Dominic.

Brigid clutched the wooden bench as though she thought to propel herself off the seat. Noticing that, the man glanced back and forth between Brigid and Dominic. A look of realization came over his face.

"Well, isn't this a fine kettle of fish? If I'm not mistaken, you two have met before. Your pious façade is starting to tarnish, Brigid. Is this man the conductor you have been working with to steal my property? Or, perhaps, you know each other on a more intimate basis."

"How dare you say something so scandalous, Stewart," Brigid spat out.

That confirmed that the two knew each other, but Dominic still couldn't piece together why Brigid willingly left the convent with him. The man used the term conductor. *Was he referring to the* Underground Railroad? If that was the case, the property he was talking about was slaves. *Were the Negroes he saw on the McGinnis property the fugitives of which the man spoke?*

"The lady doth protest too much, methinks," said Stewart. "Wouldn't that be something if, not only did I track down my property tonight, but, in the process, found the abolitionist who escorted them and a federal soldier who's aiding and abetting her? This would be one for the books."

At that moment, Brigid pushed herself down from the carriage. She hit the ground, but the echo of the hammer of a gun being clicked into place stopped her dead in her tracks. Both she and Dominic pivoted their heads towards Stewart. The derringer in his hand glinted in the moonlight.

"I wouldn't do that if I were you, Brigid. You sold your soul to me tonight, and the only way you're getting out of it is if some tragedy would befall you." Stewart edged towards the passenger side of the vehicle and then bounded down to ground level. Keeping the derringer in his right hand, he bent and grabbed Brigid's upper arm with his left. He yanked her to her feet and dragged her to the front of the horses.

With no impediments between himself and Stewart, Dominic was sorely tempted to grab his pistol. His hand hovered above the holster.

"Don't even think about it, Yank."

Pulling Brigid in close, he pressed the barrel of his gun to her right temple. "You make one wrong move, and she's gone. This one's a tasty-looking morsel but there are plenty of young women who'd come swimming around given the right bait. Besides, if she dies, then she reneges on our agreement and I get my property back from the sisters. I doubt if any of them would trade their lives for a bunch of darkies, like this sanctimonious little lady did."

Stewart pointed to Dominic. "I want you to ease that gun out of the holster and toss it into the ditch."

Reluctantly, Dominic did as he was told. Stewart then released his grip on Brigid's arm and pulled the veil off her head. He interlaced his fingers in her hair and snapped her head back.

"How about we give your beau a little entertainment before he heads off to his eternal reward?" His lips brushed Brigid's cheek, and she shivered in revulsion.

"No," she screamed, wrenching her head back as far from him as she could.

Knowing it would do no good to react rashly, Dominic held himself in check as he assessed the situation. He started counting down from five, with the thought of springing into action when he hit one. After marking off three numbers, something caught his eye. Movement came from the underside of the carriage. A dark figure crept from behind the vehicle and stealthily approached Stewart and Brigid. In a flash, a man grabbed Stewart's right arm and twisted it behind his back. A gunshot sounded.

Seeing blood on Brigid's gray smock, Dominic sprinted to her. Meanwhile, the man — a huge Negro — wrapped his free arm around Stewart's neck. He had the man in the crook of his elbow and forced the appendage down in one quick motion. A horrendous sound reverberated through the still night air — the sound of Stewart's neck snapping.

He keeled over dead.

Brigid's eyes rolled up and her face drained of all color. Dominic was there in time to catch her before she followed

Stewart to the ground. He swept her up into his arms and looked her over to assess her injuries. He saw no frayed fabric, just blood on her dress.

He then turned to the black man. The giant staggered backwards three steps and fell to the ground, clutching his thigh.

Turning in Dominic's arms, Brigid witnessed the same thing. She freed herself from his grip, dropped to the ground and ran towards the black man. She fell to her knees before him. "Good Lord, it's Marcus."

Chapter XXXI

Between watching the blood that seeped from Marcus' leg, the ghastly sight of Stewart's mangled body, and seeing Dominic dressed as a Union Army soldier, Brigid was in a state of shock.

While the option of sinking into a pool of tears held some appeal, she needed to take action. She got back on her feet, hiked her skirt up to her knees, grabbed onto the shift beneath it, and ripped off the bottom six inches of fabric. Dropping to the ground again, she wrapped the fabric around Marcus' leg. The spot where the bullet entered his thigh was obvious, but Brigid needed to determine the extent of his injury — she would have to feel the back of his leg to see if the bullet had exited.

As her hands touched the bloody fabric of his trousers, she held her breath to keep the bile from creeping up the back of her throat. It didn't take more than a few seconds of searching with her fingertips until she felt a hole in the fabric, directly over a break in his skin on the back of his thigh. That meant the shot went clear through his leg. *Thank you, Lord.* If it had been lodged in there, they'd have to get him to a doctor before gangrene set in. That could cause him to lose his leg, or even worse, his life.

Meanwhile, Dominic took charge of disposing of Stewart's body. Brigid watched as he picked up the man's feet by the boot heels and walked backwards to the ditch. It seemed to take a tremendous amount of effort to move the body. The strain caused sweat to drip unchecked down Dominic's forehead, yet he continued on until the corpse was through the ditch and several feet into the woods.

There was no way of guessing how many lives would be

spared with Stewart dead, but Brigid still felt a sense of sorrow as she watched Dominic concealing the body with sticks and leaves. Even if the man was a monster, he had a mother who saw nothing but good in him and would be worried to death when he didn't return to the plantation. Brigid crossed herself and said a quick prayer for the repose of his soul. The end came so quickly for him that he had no time to repent or make amends for the wrongdoings in his life — only the Lord knew where he'd end up.

Other than praying, she could do nothing else for him. At the present moment, she needed to concentrate on the folks who were living and wanted to maintain that status. They needed to get back to the convent so Marcus could be reunited with his family. Arrangements would need to be made for them to make their way to the next station as soon as possible. It would not be safe to stay in Cartersville too long. Stewart may have shared his plans with other slave patrollers, who could be on their way to the town at this very moment, for all she knew.

She was in a pickle herself. The patrollers didn't think too highly of folks who helped fugitives. She didn't know if Stewart had implicated her to any of his associates, but she wasn't of the mind to stick around Cartersville to find out.

Brigid completed the bandaging while Dominic walked back to the carriage, wiping his hands on his trousers. He then went to Marcus and helped him up from the ground. The big man leaned on him as they took the four steps to the conveyance. Once there, Dominic laced his fingers together and had Marcus step into the makeshift stirrup and hoist himself onto the wooden floor. After he was secured, Dominic tied his horse to the back of the vehicle, handed Brigid up onto the bench seat, and pulled himself onto the driver's side.

They rode back to town in silence. Brigid suspected that

Dominic was waiting for her to open the conversation, but her mind was racing as she considered her next move. Never in her wildest dreams would she have imagined herself being in such a predicament.

When they got back to the convent, lights could be seen in the front windows. *They must have realized I was missing,* thought Brigid. Dominic helped her down from the carriage and then went to assist Marcus. Before she even made it to the door, the portal swung open. The light illuminated Mother Mary Catherine, and several of the sisters were peeking around her like a flock of goslings.

"Praise God, you're back," said the sister. Looking closer, she noticed the blood on Brigid's habit. "Dear Lord, are you all right?

Brigid nodded her head in the affirmative. Sister Mary Catherine stepped closer and took both of Brigid's hands in her own. "You can't imagine how many prayers have been said for your well-being since we discovered you missing." The other women bobbed their veiled heads in agreement.

Looking over Brigid's shoulder, Mother Mary Catherine noticed Dominic coming up the walk with Marcus leaning on him for support. She directed Brigid towards the other sisters and turned her attention to the two men. Her face showed concern when she saw Marcus.

"Let's get him into the convent immediately, Sergeant. We can make our introductions once we're inside."

Dominic followed the woman's command. When they were all in the building, the mother superior had him help Marcus to the nearest empty sleeping quarters. She then instructed one of the postulants to fetch Sister Mary Phillip, who was trained as a nurse.

After Marcus was settled, Mother Mary Catherine returned to the entryway. Brigid and Dominic stood there ill at ease. She looked between them, and made her assessment of the situation.

"You know each other, I assume."

"Yes, ma'am," said Dominic.

"Would this by any chance be the someone who has caused you to reconsider taking religious vows, Miss McGinnis?"

Dominic's head swiveled towards Brigid. In turn, Brigid turned to him and mouthed the words, "We need to talk."

She wouldn't dare lie to a nun, but she wasn't prepared to share the details of her relationship with Dominic so she opted to do the prudent thing and delay the conversation. "If you wouldn't mind, Mother Mary Catherine, may I have a moment alone with the gentleman?" asked Brigid politely.

The nun raised her eyebrows but gave Brigid permission with a nod of her head. She then turned and left the area.

Once alone, Brigid pivoted and looked directly at Dominic. "Sergeant... Is it Warner?"

"Yes, Miss McGinnis," said Dominic, copying her formal address.

"Shall I assume you have all your faculties intact, Sergeant Warner?"

"You may," he replied.

"That is certainly good to hear. Can you enlighten me as to when your memory returned?"

"To be honest, it was about two days after we first met," replied Dominic.

She sucked in a breath, aware that her expression must've revealed a look of surprise. "Honest? I'm not so sure about that. Was there some reason you withheld that information from me at the time?"

"Yes," said Dominic, drawing the word out. "I didn't want you to know." He gave her a matter-of-fact look.

Well, that explained that. But it wasn't what she wanted to hear.

"For goodness sakes, why wouldn't you want me to know?" she asked in an exasperated voice.

"Because if you had known that my memory was restored, you would have wanted to know my background and how I ended up in your side yard. For your safety and mine, I thought it best to keep you in the dark."

Brigid crossed her arms and tapped her foot on the wooden floor. She looked at Dominic askance.

"I truly believed that after we parted ways that last evening, we would never set eyes on each other again," he explained, shrugging.

Speaking of eyes, she couldn't take hers off him.

"Fair enough," she said, finding her voice again. "Let's move to the next topic, shall we? Why are you wearing a Union Army uniform? The light may have been limited when we encountered each other previously, but I know you were dressed in gray trousers and a jacket adorned with the Confederate States of America insignia. Are you masquerading as a Union Soldier?"

"That's another excellent question, Miss McGinnis. Would you care to take a seat before I answer?"

"I'm seventeen years old, a grown woman — I'm sure I can handle whatever you have to tell me."

Dominic looked duly impressed.

"Well, here goes. When we first met, I *was* a Confederate soldier. At the time I didn't know how or why, because I wasn't even aware that our country was at war. But as the hours wore on, snippets of my life came back to me — some of which I shared with you."

Brigid nodded. Heat slipped up her neck as she recalled

those intimate conversations — and the comfort she found in his arms.

"Continue."

"The biggest revelation was when I remembered I hadn't joined the Confederate Army voluntarily — I was conscripted against my will. At the time of my conscription, I was living in a slave-holding state, but as a native of Illinois, I was a Unionist."

An unbidden gasp came from Brigid. She covered her mouth and staggered back a step.

"Are you sure you don't want that chair?" Dominic asked solicitously.

"I'm fine," Brigid whispered. In reality, she didn't know if she was fine at all. Her father would be livid if he learned that she was involved in any way with a Unionist. He had made his opinion of those misguided people very clear and was adamant that every one of them should be strung up.

"Have you joined the side of General Grant?" she asked.

He nodded.

"How was that possible?"

"I owe my thanks to Father O'Reilly — he was able to set me up with civilian clothing, escort me safely into one of the Union camps, and start the enlistment process."

The pieces were falling into place for Brigid.

"How did you end up in Cartersville?"

"By chance, I was on patrol with a fellow soldier in the area. We split up to scout the town, looking for Rebel activity. It was purely coincidental that I came upon the church and saw your interaction with Stewart."

Brigid shook her head in dissension. "It was no coincidence — it was divine intervention."

Chapter XXXII

Dominic cocked his eyebrow and looked directly at Brigid. "Divine intervention?"

"Yes. I was praying to Saint Brigid, my patron saint. I was named after her because I was born on her feast day, the first day of February, so I've sought her intercession my whole life. The dear saint sent you to rescue me."

That declaration certainly got his attention.

"As you probably gathered from the brief encounter you had with Stewart, I was willingly going back to his plantation in Dallas, because we had struck up an agreement."

"An agreement?" questioned Dominic. He couldn't imagine what possible agreement would make Brigid leave the safety of the convent and travel anywhere with that deplorable snake.

"Yes." She sighed and lowered her gaze. "I agreed to become his wife in order to save the lives of the five slaves whom I had ferried to this convent."

Two thoughts immediately came to Dominic upon hearing that. Primarily, it was a good thing that Stewart was already dead or he'd tear him apart limb by limb. He couldn't stomach the image of that creature touching Brigid. The second thought startled him, but after recalling the night he had seen the Negroes on the McGinnis property, it could make sense.

"Are you a conductor on the Underground Railroad?" he asked with a hint of admiration in his voice. There was definitely more to this girl than he could have guessed — he prayed someday he'd have the opportunity to discover all the facets of her personality.

"It depends how you look at it," said Brigid hesitantly. "Really all I was trying to do was help the folks I discovered hiding on our land. They were in such a desperate situation; I wouldn't have felt right leaving them to fend for themselves."

He couldn't help himself. Dominic took two steps forward and engulfed Brigid in his arms. "You have such a Christ-like love for humanity. How many people would be willing to give up their lives to save another fellow human being?" He gave her a squeeze. "Who couldn't love a person like you?"

She pulled her head back from his chest and looked up at him.

"What are you saying?"

"I'm saying, *Ich liebe dich, Schatzie.*" He cupped her chin with his right hand. "I love you, sweetheart, and there's nothing you can do about it."

Brigid looked at him incredulously. "*Schatzie*? I'm your sweetheart?"

"You surely are, and, God willing, someday you'll be my wife."

She blinked back tears. "How is that ever going to happen? Our country is torn apart by war, you have a commitment to serve the Union Army, Stewart's minions could be on their way to apprehend me as we speak, and I am in the middle of discerning a religious vocation."

"You *were* in the middle of discerning a religious vocation," corrected Dominic.

"I *was*." Brigid blushed as she admitted it. "But that doesn't change the other circumstances. What are we to do?"

Dominic considered that question for a moment. He

stepped back, grabbed her shoulders and gazed into her eyes.

"The item of utmost priority is your safety, young lady. We need to get you out of here immediately. Perhaps Mother Mary Catherine would know of another convent that would take you in until everything settles down. If Major General William T. Sherman carries out his threat to bring Georgia to its knees, this war could be over in less than a year, however, that might not bode well for the people of this state. You'd be best to look at heading somewhere further west, perhaps Arkansas."

"Oh my goodness, I remember my father telling me that the Sisters of Mercy has a Motherhouse in Little Rock," said Brigid.

"We should be able to book passage on a train between here and there relatively easy, assuming the Union Army hasn't played havoc with those train tracks yet. I've got some Greenbacks on me that should cover the fare — that will get you a lot further than The Confederate States of America dollar."

"If I do get permission from Mother Mary Catherine to travel to Little Rock, what will become of you then?" Brigid asked with concern in her voice.

"As soon as I leave this building, I will go to the meeting spot I established with the officer who accompanied me here tonight. After we get some rest, we will return to our regiment to await our next mission. Then I'll go back to the front or wherever I'm assigned." Brigid nodded but still looked apprehensive.

"Our number one priority while we're apart is to stay alive and stay safe. Agreed?"

"Absolutely," said Brigid. "But I fear it will take more effort for you to keep up your end of the bargain than for me to keep up mine."

"That's just as I would have it," said Dominic.

He stepped forward and wrapped her in his arms again. *If only I could freeze time*, he thought, *I would never let go of this girl again*. Dominic held her tightly — he wanted to imprint the feel of her frame in his arms, breathe in her scent and memorize her beautiful face, the striking hair, her enchanting eyes...

"Hmph."

The sound of someone intruding on their embrace immediately caused the two of them to disengage and step apart from each other.

Mother Mary Catherine tilted her chin down and peered at the couple over the top of her spectacles.

"Unless there is a promise of upcoming nuptials betwixt the two of you, it would be a good idea for you to refrain from physical contact," said the sister. "The spirit is willing, but the flesh is weak, as Saint Mark reminds us."

Dominic heard the woman loud and clear. He reached out to Brigid and engulfed her right hand with his two hands. She looked at him as if he had lost his mind once again. Then she inclined her head slightly toward Mother Mary Catherine and tried to pull her hand away, but he wouldn't let go.

"Brigid," he said, feeling her hand trembling under his. "I promise to you, before God and his most gracious advocate, Mother Mary Catherine, that when this war is over, I will find you and take you to be my wife, if you'll have me for your husband."

All Brigid could do was nod *yes*. Tears trickled down her cheeks.

"How's that, Mother?"

"Magnificent, young man."

With the sister's blessing taken care of, Dominic got up, grabbed Brigid around the waist, and swirled her around. Once she had her feet back on the floor, he gave her another hug, planted a chaste kiss on her forehead and reluctantly let her go.

"Mother Mary Catherine, here are all the Greenbacks I have. Can you get Brigid on the next train to Little Rock? She tells me there is another motherhouse for the Sisters of Mercy there. If you can use your influence to secure a spot there for her until I get back, I would be greatly obliged to you."

"I'm sure that can be arranged, Sergeant."

"If there is any extra money, give it to Marcus, to help him and his family on their passage out of the South."

"I will do that."

"Brigid," he said, turning his attention to her. "This is probably the hardest thing I'll ever have to do, but I must leave now. Sergeant Magie will put out a search party for me if I don't show up at our designated meeting place, and before you know it, the entire 2nd Brigade 2nd Division XIV Corps, 78th Illinois Volunteer Infantry Regiment will be turning this town upside down looking for me. You take care of yourself, promise?"

She managed to nod in agreement.

Dominic took one last glance at her. Then he opened the door and walked outside, closing the door quietly behind him. Heaving a sigh, he took a few steps towards the street. He then heard the handle on the door click. Before he knew it, someone was behind him.

He immediately sensed it was Brigid. Before he could react, she scooted in front of him and threw her arms around his waist.

"You have to promise me, Sergeant Dominic Warner,

that you will come back to me," she said firmly, looking up at him.

"I will try my very best, *Schatzie*."

"Trying isn't good enough, you have to do it." She released her hold on him and then reached up and gripped the points of his shirt collar in her clenched fingers. "If you don't come back to me, I will be making my vows with the Sisters of Mercy."

She stood on her tiptoes, pulled his face next to hers, and firmly planted a kiss on his lips. "If I can't have you, I don't want anybody."

Chapter XXXIII

Brigid gazed out the window of the train heading west. She held a letter of passage from Mother Mary Catherine that she was to present to the mother superior of the Little Rock Sisters of Mercy Convent. Should she be stopped by any soldiers along the trip, it would also serve as validation of her travel destination.

Other than the conductor, Brigid interacted with no one on the train. The other passengers seemed to be of no mood to converse, which suited her just fine. She just wanted to make it to the convent, get settled in, and find a way to bide her time until the hostilities between the states ceased and Dominic would come for her.

The Sisters of Mercy house was walking distance from the train station, so there was no need to hire a hansom cab to get there. Mother Mary Catherine had given her one of Dominic's Greenbacks in case she needed money, but Brigid was determined not to spend that dollar. It was the only physical link she had between Dominic and herself.

The Little Rock mother superior welcomed her as a postulant without reviewing her resume. Who knew, with the war going on, perhaps they were willing to take unscreened candidates or, maybe the letter from Mother Mary Catherine compelled her to take on a new postulant, no questions asked. Having been accustomed to the routine in Cartersville, Brigid fell right in line with the Little Rock postulants. They began their day at five-thirty in the morning with Adoration of the Blessed Sacrament, followed by Morning Prayer, Mass and breakfast. At nine o'clock, the sisters went out into the community, ministering to the sick and poor, while the postulants stayed at the convent for classes. Communal Prayer began at noon, lunch was at one, and additional classes were conducted in the afternoon. Adoration of the Blessed Sacrament began at five o'clock and the Rosary was recited afterward. The evening meal was served at six. After chores, the women had free time. Night Prayer started at eight thirty, and lights were out at nine o'clock — which began twelve hours of silence in the house.

On Sundays, they were given time off from classes to attend Mass and spend their time in prayer. Outside of class hours, Wednesdays and Fridays passed in silence. Those days were also set aside for fasting.

Prayer in their community was never-ending. On one hand, Brigid found it ideal because it gave her the chance to pray for Dominic's safety. She had no need to pray for herself — nothing caused her to feel unsafe on the grounds of the convent. The only thing that could kill her at this point was boredom. Going through the same routine day in and day out was tedious, to say the least. She didn't know how the other girls felt about it, but it was maddening for her.

The postulants were allowed to leave the convent grounds once a week. Brigid stuck close to the cocoon of the convent — she was still leery of encountering any of Stewart's associates.

On Saturday afternoons, the girls had the option to use their free time to pray, pursue a pastime such as embroidery — altar cloths and handkerchiefs were popular items to work on — or get outside for fresh air and a walk, as long as they stayed in groups. Brigid had plenty of prayer time during the week, and she wasn't all that interested in needlework — she'd done her share of it at the Lucy Cobb Institute. She generally opted to sit in the fenced in back garden and think.

Of course, most of the time, her mind turned to Dominic. She wondered where he was and how he fared. At times she thought of her parents and her little sisters. As far as they knew, she still lived in Cartersville under the wing of Mother Mary Catherine. As the war went on, was her father spending extra time with his government duties or was he trying to be more attentive to his family and the household since she was no longer there to help? Perhaps her mother was over her spell and was able to take charge of her duties once again. Were the girls applying themselves to their studies?

Thinking of her father, she wondered how he would react when she found out that she was, in essence, betrothed to a man who hadn't even asked his permission to court her. There was no going back now, but she would feel better if, someday, she and Dominic were to receive her father's blessing.

The fact that Dominic fought for the Union Army may be a sticking point. *Actually, it would definitely be a sticking point.* But the war couldn't go on forever. Maybe once a truce was drawn, all hostilities would be set aside. Unfortunately, that notion seemed farfetched. Her father, for one, held onto grudges tighter than a miser holds onto pennies.

It took until the beginning of autumn before Brigid got the nerve to venture off the property. She finally felt the threat of retribution from the event with Stewart had passed. Little news of the war reached the ears of the postulants. For most of them, it was probably a blessing, but Brigid was anxious to find out anything she could about Dominic's regiment.

One Saturday afternoon, she was able to persuade a couple of fellow postulants to walk with her to the general store. They had no money to spend, but she convinced them that it would be interesting to look around and see what products were available. Who knew, maybe the shopkeeper would feel kindly towards them and offer them a piece of stick candy for free.

When they got to the store, the other girls went to the glass case to admire the candy flavors while Brigid went to the back of the building to see if the shopkeeper had any recent newspapers. She was in luck; he had stacks of the weekly paper, going back several months. She asked if it would be permissible to look through them. He readily agreed, even though by his look, he wondered why they would be of interest to her.

Brigid memorized Dominic's regiment when he had mentioned it the last time they were together — Union Army, 2nd Brigade, 2nd Division, XIV Corps — the 78th Illinois Volunteer Infantry Regiment. Starting with the paper from the week after she had last seen Dominic, she quickly scanned each periodical for any news of the Union Army, 2nd Brigade. Surprisingly, she saw more mention of it than she anticipated. It was a broad category, so there was no guarantee that the 78th Illinois was involved in any listed engagements, but at least she had some idea of their movements.

The 2nd Brigade had fought battles at Pine Mountain, Lost Mountain and Kennesaw Mountain. The brigade participated in an unsuccessful and costly assault on the Confederate position on Cheatham Hill. Brigid prayed that Dominic was not one of the many casualties from that affair. There were engagements in other places she had never heard of, like Ruff's Station, and skirmishes near bodies of water like the Chattahoochee River, Peach Tree Creek and Utoy Creek.

The Battle of Atlanta began the fifth of August and lasted three days. That news was unfavorable for the Confederate States, because Atlanta was said to be one of their last strongholds. The headline for the newspaper dated the second week in September declared that Atlanta had fallen to Union troops on the second of September. It wasn't clear if the 2nd Division was part of that momentous day because there had also been engagement battle at Lovejoy Station that same week, and they were listed as being part of that.

It was heartening to see any news of the 2nd Brigade, but only the Lord knew how the Illinois 78th was holding out. Regardless of her father's stance, she was glad Dominic was fighting for the Union forces. From what she read, the Federal forces had the upper hand at this point. That comforted her. In her heart, Brigid believed that the man she loved was still alive and fighting to get back to her.

The postulants were rewarded with their stick candy that day, so Brigid figured it wouldn't be too difficult to coerce them to accompany her to the general store again sometime. She didn't want it to be too obvious that she was tracking news of the war — after all, their mission was to be in the world, not of the world, so she held herself in check and went to the store only once a month.

As the year wore on, the postulants continued to march through their routine and advance in their studies. Just like the seasons of the year came one after another, so did the seasons of the Church. Ordinary Time was followed by Advent which led up to Christmas. It was a bright spot during the gloomy month of December.

On that day, they followed the Morning Prayer as usual, but the finishing touch on their breakfast plate was a slice of heavenly fruit cake. After that, mail was delivered to a number of the women, one piece at a time. To her surprise, Brigid received a letter from her mother. It was the only contact the postulants were allowed with their family until the day they made their vows as novitiates in June.

Brigid noticed that the envelope was addressed to the Mother House in Cartersville. She was grateful it had been forwarded to her in Little Rock. Reading the two-sided letter, she struggled to keep her tears in check. She missed her family and was nostalgic for life back in her hometown. Of course, life would never be the way it once was, but her mother was sensitive enough to write a lighthearted note and gloss over any hardships that they may have been facing.

How Brigid's heart yearned for correspondence from Dominic. Even if he had the opportunity to write to her, she doubted he had the skills to pen anything in English. But she would have been more than happy to receive any note from him, even if it was written in German.

After Christmas came The Solemnity of the Mother of God on the first day of the new year. Brigid wondered what 1865 would hold for her.

Epiphany was the last Church holiday before they went back to Ordinary Time. Ash Wednesday, which marked the beginning of Lent, fell on the first day of March.

By April, springtime was in full bloom and Lent was more than halfway over. Everyone in the Motherhouse anticipated Easter, which was on the sixteenth of the month. The city of Little Rock seemed to be awakening as well. As hard as it was for those loyal to the Southern cause to admit, it was inevitable that the Confederate Army faced defeat. But, after four years of fighting, hardships, and the loss of so many of their young men, most citizens were ready to be done with the war which had divided their country and disrupted so many lives.

On the ninth of April, a telegram was sent to Arkansas governor Harris Flanagin, proclaiming that General Robert E. Lee surrendered the Army of Northern Virginia to Lieutenant General Ulysses S. Grant at Appomattox Court House in Appomattox, Virginia. It was the beginning of the end of the war.

The 2nd Brigade had apparently accompanied General William T. Sherman on his March to the Sea, leaving a path of destruction behind from Atlanta to Savannah. Brigid hoped Dominic wasn't part of that, but she knew, as a soldier, he would have to do what he was ordered to do. It appeared that they were then sent to the Carolinas on another campaign. There was no telling where they were now or if they even knew of Lee's surrender.

Not even one week later, the news erupted that President Abraham Lincoln was assassinated. Regardless of what her father had said about him, Brigid held no animosity towards the man. Now that she was keeping abreast of the national news, she had been hopeful that he would help bring their nation back together.

Day after day, more Southern generals, troops, states, and territories surrendered to the Union. Regiments were beginning to disband, and soldiers were being mustered out of the service by the hundreds.

As the time crept closer to June, Brigid was having serious concerns about Dominic. The men in the Illinois 78th should have been sent back home by now.

Looking out the window one day, Brigid admired the beautiful flowers lining the perimeter of the convent. The forget-me-nots, snapdragons and poppies, which the sisters planted during the Month of Mary, were already blossoming.

Someone approached her from behind. Brigid was so lost in thought, she didn't notice until the woman cleared her throat.

"Any word yet?"

The familiar voice startled her. Brigid swung around with a look of astonishment on her face.

"Mother Mary Catherine!" she exclaimed. Disregarding

protocol, she threw herself into the sister's arms.

"I never thought I'd see you again, Mother." Tears clouded her eyes as she pulled back and looked at the mother superior. "What brings you to Little Rock?"

"I am accompanying our postulants from Cartersville. They will be making their vows with the group of young ladies here."

Brigid wasn't aware of that arrangement. "It will be nice seeing the girls again," she said sincerely. "But why aren't they making their vows at your parish?"

"The Diocese of Little Rock has been without a bishop since their beloved Bishop Andrew Byrne passed away. The state of Georgia is under the leadership of Bishop Augustin Verot of the Diocese of Savannah. Bishop Verot is conducting the veiling ceremony for the Sister of Mercy postulants in Georgia and Arkansas. It was his wish to combine the sisters for one ceremony," she explained.

That would certainly make sense, Brigid thought. Most likely the decision was made months ago when Georgia was still under siege by General Sherman.

"Fate has brought us together again, Mother Mary Catherine. I truly am happy to see you. Can you tell me what has become of Alice and her family?"

"I'm glad to report that they have reached their destination safely."

"Praise God," said Brigid. It was a relief to know they were out of harm's way.

"And how about you, Brigid. Have you heard anything of Dominic?"

"No, Mother." She turned her attention back to the flowers to hide the sorrow she knew her face showed.

"You've only ten days until the veil ceremony."

Brigid nodded.

"I've been praying for his safe return."

"Thank you, Mother."

"His fate is in God's hands."

Once again, Brigid nodded. The lump in her throat made it impossible to speak.

"It's been six weeks since the terms of surrender were signed." The woman hesitated. "It is proper to hold onto hope, but you need to be realistic as well. As painful as it may be, a decision must be made soon on how you will go forward with your life."

A tear slipped down Brigid's cheek. "I know, Mother," she choked out.

"Brigid, God has a vocation for you. But it's up to you to discern whether it's the religious life, married life or single life," said the sister. "We welcome you to become a full member of our community, but becoming a sister should not be a contingency plan for your life — it should be the only plan."

"I understand."

"Look to your patron saint for guidance. She'll steer you in the right direction."

"I will. Thank you for the advice, Mother."

That thought stayed with Brigid through the next week as final preparations were made for the veiling ceremony. Each time she stopped in the chapel, she appealed to Saint Brigid for guidance. The words mentioned about discernment kept swirling through her mind.

The Taking of the Veil ceremony was to be held during Mass on Sunday, the eighteenth of June, at Saint Andrew's Cathedral on the corner of Second Street and Center Street in Little Rock.

The Friday before the ceremony, all of the veiling

candidates gathered in the chapel. Mother Teresa Farrell went over the final details of the event.

"It's a blessing to take your vows on the feast day of Saint Marina Virgin," she noted. "Like you, she chose the life of a religious. But," the sister paused for effect, "she served God under the habit of a monk." Several young ladies gasped.

"It really is quite extraordinary. However, what made Saint Marina remarkable was her wonderful humility, meekness and patience. Those are traits to emulate in your vocation."

Throughout her life, people had attributed those characteristics to Brigid. Perhaps this was the sign she was looking for. Was God nudging her to profess her final vows?

By now, the troops on either side of the conflict had been mustered out of the service. No matter where Dominic may have been at the conclusion of the war, it wouldn't take more than four weeks to get to Little Rock, even if he traveled by foot.

The Lord giveth and the Lord taketh away. God had a purpose for placing Dominic in her life. While it could have been for a number of reasons, two came immediately to Brigid's mind — the opportunity to experience unconditional love and the chance to learn to forgive herself.

Now, it appeared that God had called Dominic home — her path was clear.

Two days later, Brigid looked over the new habit laid out on her bed. She smoothed down the fabric and thought about the upcoming ceremony. Her heart was heavy. A psalm she memorized came to mind, "*He gathers together the exiles of Israel, healing the broken-hearted and binding up their wounds.*"

Perhaps if her family was in Little Rock for the ceremony, she wouldn't feel so melancholy. Most of the other girls would have loved ones in attendance, but her father couldn't break away from work to make the trip with her family. With the war over, he needed to get the bank running shipshape once again. Besides, she wasn't sure how she felt about him after it was confirmed that he was involved in the slave trade.

In a letter Brigid received several days earlier, her mother assured her that they would correspond as often as they were allowed to and, when things settled down, would come visit her even if she landed as far away as the motherhouse in San Francisco.

Maybe after that much time had passed, Brigid would then be able to face her father.

Steeling herself, Brigid swiftly pulled the old habit off. She folded it neatly, laid it on the bed, and put the white habit on. The decision was made — her vocation was to give her life to Jesus.

In a short while, she would be betrothed again. She and the other postulants were accepting the call to become brides of Christ. As novitiates, they would be veiled in black, and, in three years, when they professed their final vows, they would be adorned in black from head to toe.

Leaving her room, Brigid saw the other young ladies going down the hall in the direction of the foyer. There was a sense of giddiness about them. They chattered back and forth in excitement. She hid the dour expression on her face and quickened her pace to catch up with them.

After a short drive to the cathedral, the postulants disembarked from the carriages. They were awestruck as they looked up at the imposing building. A hush fell on them and they folded their hands in reverence before walking through the oversized wooden doors.

Once inside the church, they dipped their fingers in holy water and made the Sign of the Cross. Then they formed a single file line, shortest to tallest, and processed to the assigned pews in the front. Brigid was the first in line. She genuflected before making her way to the end of the pew. They knelt in prayer as the bells rang for the call to Mass.

When Brigid spied Bishop Verot lined up with other clergy in the back of the church, the reality of the situation hit her. But, at that moment, a sense of calm enveloped her. In her heart, she knew she was precisely where God wanted her to be.

Mass began, and Brigid did everything she could to keep her mind focused on the proceedings. She would want to remember this day forever. As the service wound down, the postulants stood and processed to the altar. They each took their assigned spot at the altar kneelers.

When the bishop waved his hand, they knelt as a group before him. One at a time, a professed sister walked up behind a postulant and placed a black veil on top of her bowed head. After the veil was placed, Bishop Verot said a blessing over the novitiate.

Sliding her eyes to the left, Brigid watched the bishop draw nearer. She swallowed hard when he stopped directly in front of her. Footsteps sounded from the back of the church, and her anticipation heightened as they got closer.

The church grew eerily silent. Brigid looked up at Bishop Verot. He nodded in approval to the person behind her. She felt the veil being placed on her head. It was much lighter than she anticipated.

Holding her breath, she glanced down at the fabric lying against her shoulder. Her eyes widened in shock and her mouth gaped open. It was a veil, but it wasn't the one she expected to see. She blinked to make sure her eyes weren't playing tricks on her in the dim light.

The veil wasn't black cotton fabric like the ones that the other young ladies were given. Rather, it was white gossamer fabric edged with lace.

Brigid stared at the bishop. He smiled at her and inclined his head to the person standing behind her. She twisted around to see.

An audible gasp escaped her lips. Her body went numb. She couldn't believe her eyes. It was not a professed sister behind her, but rather, a man. A very handsome one at that — a sergeant wearing full regalia Union blues. He smiled at her tenderly.

She looked at him incredulously. "Dominic?"

He reached down and clasped her left hand in his. "I told you I would be back, didn't I?"

Brigid nodded, still in a state of astonishment.

Dominic dropped down on one knee to the floor and, with Brigid on the kneeler, he was nearly eye-level with her.

"This time we'll make it formal, *Schatzie*." He reached into his pocket and pulled out a simple gold band.

"Brigid McGinnis, I knew from the moment I first laid eyes on you that I would love you until the end of my life. Through the intervention of the angels and saints who've been watching over me these last several months, and by God's will — my life has been spared. Sheer determination to see you again kept me going when I didn't think I could make it anymore. Will you do me the honor of becoming my wife?"

Tears caught on her lower lashes, but Brigid saw clearly enough to witness the love in Dominic's eyes. It reflected the love in her heart.

"Becoming your wife will be the greatest blessing I've ever received. The answer is yes, Dominic, I will."

"There's no time like the present. Bishop Verot, seeing that we're in this holy cathedral, would you do us the honor of joining us in marriage today?"

"It would be my pleasure," said the older man. "This day shall be doubly blessed. But first, let us offer the closing prayer over our novitiates."

Dominic placed the ring back in his trouser pocket, stood and helped Brigid to her feet. Hand in hand, they stepped back a respectful distance. As Bishop Verot conferred his final blessing on the young women, Brigid did everything she could to control her tears. Apparently, she wasn't the only one — she could hear sniffles throughout the cathedral. Several nuns dabbed their eyes with daintily-embroidered handkerchiefs.

Brigid looked down at Dominic's strong hand engulfing hers. As she thought of how God brought her to this moment, her gratitude knew no bounds. To think — she had been moments away from dedicating her life to the Church. Now she would be dedicating her life to Dominic. Her heart was bursting with joy.

Dominic touched her chin and tilted her head back.

"Who would have thought a year ago that this is how our lives would have turned out?" he whispered.

Brigid smiled and squeezed his hand. "I'm grateful that we were open to God's plan, rather than trying to force our own plans upon Him. He always knows the greater good."

"I'm not sure what I did to deserve you, Brigid, but I'm glad God sought fit to bring you into my life."

"I could say the same thing, Dominic." Tears trickled down her cheeks. She looked up at the stained-glass windows. While her tears blurred the sight, she could make out the depiction of the Blessed Mother at the Annunciation — on the eve of her own marriage.

"Thank you, Blessed Mother," Brigid murmured. She then turned her full attention to the man who would soon be her husband.

Epilogue

The wedding ceremony was short and simple but an event Brigid would never forget. Dominic had arranged everything ahead of time, so that when the couple emerged hand-in-hand from the cathedral after their nuptials, two horses and a covered wagon waited for them. To her surprise, Dominic had stopped at the Motherhouse in Cartersville and picked up one of her trunks. It contained the hodgepodge of clothing and personal items she had grabbed when she left Dallas all those months ago. But, at least it gave her something to wear other than the white habit.

As for that piece of clothing, she intended to keep it — after all, it was her wedding gown, and, who knew, maybe someday she could use the fabric to make a baptismal gown, if she and Dominic were blessed with children.

Their honeymoon consisted of traveling three hundred miles back to the ranch Dominic owned with Nathan. With their team of horses, they were able to go about twenty-five miles per day, so they would reach their destination in two weeks. On the way, they stopped at a small town and Brigid was able to post a letter to her family informing them of her change in circumstances. She kept the details to a minimum and let them know where she and Dominic would be settling.

It wasn't a fancy honeymoon by any means, but it was exactly what she and Dominic needed — time to get to know each other better. Dominic had so many tales to share from his childhood, his years working on farms, and building his ranching enterprise with Nathan. Brigid could listen to him for hours on end. She especially loved his wit. It was woven throughout his stories. He could find humor in just about any situation. Dominic skimmed over details of the atrocities of war but made her laugh when he talked about the various characters in his regiment. A number of narratives were about the country bumpkin Danny and how it turned into almost a full-time job keeping the lad alive until the war finally came to a close.

For Brigid, the more she learned about Dominic, the more she loved him. His words and actions made it obvious that the feeling was mutual. Nearing his property was bittersweet — she was going to miss having him all to herself. Brigid turned and looked over the wagon that had been their living area the past fortnight. It was tight quarters, but it was all theirs. She smiled when she recalled Dominic carrying her up the back two steps the first night of their marriage to cross the threshold of the wagon. "If we're going to start our marriage here, we ought to make it official," he said, giving her a wink.

When they crested the last hill before Dominic's ranch, Brigid put her hand in his and held on tight. He had described the land and the buildings in detail and told her about the people who lived and worked on the ranch, including Nathan and his wife, Mrs. Simmons. Brigid was anxious to meet the young lady. Dominic didn't know much about her because they had only met briefly at the ranch before he returned to Arkansas.

***

After the war ended, Dominic's regiment had been assigned to occupy the city of Raleigh, the capital of North Carolina. On the twenty-sixth of April, he was present at Bennett Place in Durham for the largest surrender of Confederate soldiers ever — which many considered to be the official end of the war.

Like a number of other troops, the Illinois 78th was ordered to march to Washington, D.C., for the Grand Review. As much of an honor as it would have been for Dominic to see President Andrew Johnson, he asked for permission to resign his commission immediately in Raleigh, so he could return to Texas to see what had become of his ranch and the people living there.

The soldiers of the Illinois 78th were scheduled to be mustered out the first week of June, but Dominic was given an honorable discharge on the twenty-seventh of April. Before he took leave of his commanding officers, one last time he was honored — for meritorious service in the field, he was promoted to the rank of Company Quartermaster Sergeant. Along with the new chevrons, which were hastily sewn onto his jacket by the major's wife, he was also given a cash bonus and was told he could keep the horse and firearm he had used while serving his regiment.

That mare had certainly served her purpose. She helped get Dominic through the war alive and transported him almost all the way to Texas. When they were crossing from Louisiana into Texas, Majesty threw a shoe. Dominic ended up walking the last portion of that journey with her meandering behind him.

But things happen for a reason, as they say. By chance, he encountered a soldier walking the same path. Dominic was astonished to hear the man was going to Heavenly Vista Ranch as well. It turned out he was Mrs. Simmons' brother Michael.

The man had been mustered out of the Confederate Army several weeks earlier. He went to Atlanta in search of his family, but their house was abandoned. Apparently, the only blood relative who survived the war was his sister. His old companion, Father O'Reilly of the Church of the Immaculate Conception, knew whom the girl had married and from where the man hailed. He sent the soldier off in that direction to find them.

Even though Dominic and Michael had fought on opposite sides of the war, they were able to put the hostilities behind them and developed a kinship on their trek to the ranch.

Dominic found the property in pristine condition when they arrived, just as he had hoped. Seeing Nathan alive and well was one of the best moments of his life. The reunion between Michael and his sister was touching.

As exhausted as Dominic was from his travels, he couldn't stay on the property for more than a day. He swapped out Majesty, who was officially being put to pasture, for two fresh stallions that could easily pull a covered wagon to Arkansas and back.

Those very horses and the wagon were now climbing the hill that marked the boundary of Heavenly Vista Ranch. After cresting it, they came to a halt. Dominic jumped down from the bench seat and went around the wagon to help Brigid disembark. Seeing their arrival, people rushed forward from all areas of the property to welcome Dominic back.

***

Because of Dominic's accurate narrative, everything before her on the ranch looked exactly as Brigid had pictured. The people who worked on the ranch were just as kind and gracious as he said they would be. The only two folks who weren't in the yard to greet them when they pulled up were Nathan and his wife. A few minutes later, the couple walked out of the house. Dominic had been spot on describing them as well. Nathan was tall and lean, with dark hair and a muscular build that nearly matched Dominic's. His wife was a good deal shorter than her husband but on the taller side for a woman. She was quite slender, except for her midriff section — it was apparent she was with child. Her figure was admirable, but her most striking feature was her auburn hair. It hung free and nearly touched her expanded waistline.

The sun shone directly in Brigid's face as she turned towards the couple. Shielding her eyes, she stepped away from the rest of the group to introduce herself to the man and his wife. The women looked at each other at the same time. Their initial reaction was nearly identical — each woman gasped and covered her mouth with her hand.

They stepped together and wrapped their arms around each other. Then the two of them promptly broke into tears. Their shoulders shook and they swayed back and forth. It caused an uncomfortable silence to pass through the group surrounding them.

Finally, Dominic cleared his throat to get the women's attention. They broke apart and, still sniffling, turned towards him.

"Brigid, have you met Mrs. Simmons before or is this a standard greeting for females?" he asked on behalf of all the men present.

Both women laughed.

"Dominic, I knew this young lady long before she was Mrs. Simmons. This is Amara, my best friend from my days at Lucy Cobb."

"We never imagined we'd see each other again," added Amara. The crying began anew, and the women fell back into each other's arms.

"What are the chances?" Dominic asked, a look of surprise etched on his face.

"This has to be one of the craziest coincidences I've ever heard of," echoed Nathan.

He looked back and forth between the two women, shaking his head. "Why don't you ladies go in the house and get reacquainted where it's a little cooler?"

"We'll unhitch the horses and meet you inside in a bit," added Dominic.

Amara and Brigid turned to walk arm-in-arm to the house.

"Who'd ever have thought that two best friends would marry two best friends?" said Dominic to Nathan.

"Two peas in a pod for two peas in a pod," said Nathan with a chuckle. Brigid and Amara heard his remark and laughed again.

Once inside, the women sat on the settee and conversed about what had gone on in their lives since the last time they were together. But, before they got too far into that subject, Brigid couldn't help but remark about her friend's maternal state.

"Amara, I can't tell you how happy I am that you and Nathan are expecting a baby. That child is going to be beautiful — whether she takes after you or he takes after his father. How did you feel when you found out you were expecting?"

"Oh my goodness, Brigid. Nathan and I were so excited, and we felt so blessed to be welcoming a new child into the world. It's hard to describe."

"I can imagine." She paused and took Amara's hands in her own. "What I actually want to know is, physically, how did you feel when you discovered you were with child?"

"I was tired, nauseated, and I noticed my cycle was off," Amara confided. "Is there some reason you're asking?" she asked suspiciously.

Brigid smiled widely, then stood up, pulling Amara with her. "Come back outside with me for a moment, if you will."

"Of course," Amara said enthusiastically.

The two went back through the woven wire door. The horses were unhitched and being led to the barn by one of the men. Dominic and Nathan were talking near the wagon.

Brigid and Amara walked hand-in-hand towards the two men. When they were directly in front of them, Brigid put her free hand on her friend's rounded belly. Nathan beamed with pride. Brigid then removed her hand and patted her own stomach. "Make that *three* peas in a pod for *three* peas in a pod."

In a flash, Dominic understood the implication of her words. His face broke out in a wide grin — he whooped and pulled his wife into his arms. There was a catch in his voice as he addressed Brigid.

"I have the most beautiful wife in the world, and now we're going to have a child of our own. Truly, I am lucky and blessed beyond measure."

"*We* are lucky and blessed beyond measure," said Brigid with a sense of awe in her voice. "This may not be the life that either of us planned for ourselves, but a greater power has been at work. We truly are living a life such as heaven intended."

THE END

Acknowledgements

For my husband John Lauer, our children Stephanie, Nicholas, Samantha and Elizabeth, and our entire family for their continued love and support

For Samantha Lauer, our cover model after whom the lovely and sweet Brigid is modeled

For photographer Brad Birkholz for shooting the photo of our cover model

For Sue Kiesau who provided the Civil War gown for our cover model

For Lois Gegare, hair stylist and makeup artist for our cover model

For Heritage Hill State Historical Park for providing the photo of Tank Cottage for the book cover

For James Hrkach for his work creating a book cover that is not only striking but draws the readers into this Civil War romance

For my publisher Ellen Gable Hrkach and her continued faith and confidence in me and my work

To Full Quiver Publishing for its dedication to bringing books to the public that will entertain, enlighten and bring readers closer to Christ

To all the soldiers who fought in the Civil War — all gave some; some gave all

About the Author

Wisconsin resident Amanda Lauer saw her debut novel published October 29, 2014. *A World Such as Heaven Intended* hit the number 1 spot in its genre on Amazon two months later and was the 2016 CALA winner (Young Adult). The second book in the trilogy is scheduled to be published April 5, 2018. Lauer learned the technical aspects of writing as a proofreader in the insurance, newspaper and collegiate arenas. Over the last 14 years she has had more than 1,300 articles published in newspapers and magazines throughout the United States. In addition to her proofreading, copy editing and writing career, Lauer is involved in the health and wellness industry. She and her husband John have been married 36 years, and have four grown children and four adorable grandchildren.

Published by:
Full Quiver Publishing
PO Box 244
Pakenham ON K0A2X0 Canada
www.fullquiverpublishing.com

47594195R00156

Made in the USA
Middletown, DE
08 June 2019